BRILLIANCE

BRILLIANCE

Anthony McCarten

ALMA BOOKS

ALMA BOOKS LTD
London House
243–253 Lower Mortlake Road
Richmond
Surrey TW9 2LL
United Kingdom
www.almabooks.com

Brilliance first published in Great Britain by Alma Books Limited in 2012
Copyright © Anthony McCarten, 2012
This mass-market edition first published by Alma Books Limited in 2013

Anthony McCarten asserts his moral right to be identified as the author of
this work in accordance with the Copyright, Designs and Patents Act 1988

Printed in Great Britain by CPI Group (UK) Ltd, Croydon CR0 4YY

ISBN: 978-1-84688-236-4

BRILLIANCE

A VIGNETTE

The inventor poured himself a glass of milk and listened for the twentieth century. A few seconds remained on the clock, but as part of a personal experiment he wanted to drain the milk before the first chimes of midnight.

On this night of nights he was alone in his study. His wife had sent him up to dress for the centennial celebrations about to erupt one floor below, but he had become distracted by a minor experiment. With his old Prince Albert jacket hanging limp from his shoulders and his straw hat still on his head, he craned forward, filling the glass up to a precise level marked by his thumb. Happy with the amount, he took the glass and drank with the studious concentration of an alcoholic.

And with that, just while he was smacking his lips, the Dresden wall clock struck the first note. The century was over. A sky rocket filled the window. At its zenith it exploded. Stars fell.

The century, which the *New York Times* had gone so far as to dedicate to him, naming him "its most significant contributor", was suddenly a mere anecdote. And he was pleased it was over. Hopefully, he thought, the veneration of him as a God would be over soon as well; also, the ludicrous quips that his name was so synonymous with anything new that the very idea for a new century must have come out of his laboratory. No, he wouldn't regret the closing of "the Eighteens" – good riddance. Let this new century find its new messiah.

The uproar of mirth from the rooms below only deepened his resolve not to join in the festivities. Wiping away the milk from his upper lip, he licked the tip of his pencil – his most dependable joy remained his work – and began to register the latest liquid intake against his current weight, steady at a respectable 148 pounds.

This secret test, to ascertain if it was possible for a human being to be sustained entirely by a single nutrient, in this case milk, was three weeks old, and it was reaching a crucial point. He understood that such a landmark discovery, should it even prove medically viable, would be publicly scorned and of no commercial value whatsoever. Still, the field fascinated him, and since his early days he'd been drawn to the wacky nutritional regimens of his father, an autodidact with the chin beard and naked lip of a Quaker. Also, the inventor's first wife – God rest her soul and forgive his treatment of her – had died young and perhaps from a mono-dietary intake: chocolate. Was his current experiment, then, an elaborate exhumation of his first marriage? A belated investigation, a morbid enquiry?

Rising, he found that nine paces were sufficient to take him to the bookshelf. En route he tapped the thermometer on the wall. It had been tapped too often to react in any intelligible way, and remained frozen at seven degrees Fahrenheit.

He located the book he sought. The flyleaf bore his father's faded signature. Returning to his chair, eager to read, but seeing ripples on the surface of the milk in the jug from the merriment below, he drove his heel into the floorboards. Too much noise! There was no need for such pandemonium. His phonograph was being played far too loudly. What on earth was this new century to be like? What lay in store? He was certain it would be a noisy one. And to what extent had he contributed to the noises that would be made? He often worried about how many of his inventions he would soon have to repudiate, as each was put to some abhorrent use. When he had first come up with the phonograph, purely as a business tool, he had no idea it could be used for entertainment purposes. He made a mental note to install limiters to reduce the volume output in all future phonographs, to ward against such outbreaks of frivolity.

He sat and opened the old, worn book. But he only got halfway through the first paragraph when something was smashed at the party. Didn't his family know – they certainly should by now – that even though he was virtually stone-deaf at fifty-three, utter silence, free of all audiophonic vibrations, was still vital for him to work? No one required silence more than a deaf man. The slightest tremor was an earthquake. He bent and bit the edge of his desk, sinking his teeth into the soft wood, as was his need when he wanted more phonic information (the desk's edge was already heavily chewed at that point), and with this single act he became a human amplifier. The sensitive bones of his jaw transmitted the faintest tremors so precisely he could decipher them like Morse Code, and since boyhood he had been an expert telegrapher. With the house now acting as the brass horn to a phonograph and his mandible a near-perfect sounding plate, he was able to isolate details in the general din: the shout of his youngest son, the rhythmic stamping of shoes, the fall of the glass ladle into the punchbowl, the singing of a song – what was it? He bit harder – 'Auld Lang Syne'.

Holding the old book in his thick, tradesman's hands, he flicked through to a new page and gave the smile that was the only inheritance of his Scottish Presbyterian mother. *The Temperate Life* by Luigi Cornaro, eighty-four pages in quarto, first published in 1558 when the Italian had himself been eighty-four. The book's length was no coincidence. Cornaro was an attentive numerologist, superstitious to the point of insanity, remaining in bed on all calendar days divisible by five and seven. Reading at random, Edison could hear in these kooky writings the ghostly injunctions of his father from forty years before: our acceptance of mortal death was simply a weakness of will; human longevity, like the hunt for alchemical gold, lay just over the horizon; and an abstemious diet was the first step. "You may leave the table, Alva." But Alva, fork in hand, still starving, a skinny kid to boot, told his father he wanted more. "Then this is the perfect time to leave the table, Alva. While you are still wanting more." The Dutch *Jan-Kees* knew a great deal about the pedagogic value of hunger.

The inventor soon became aware that someone was belting on the door. He rose, used nine paces to reach it, opened it briskly and was warmed by his wife's hopeful face, those slanting green eyes, the lustrous hair that requested, without a word, that he re-enter the human race. Using several of the small gestures that made up their marital sign language, she indicated that he was needed downstairs at once.

Here was the old trouble again. Interruptions, family demands, banal invasions. Was it any wonder that Alexander the Great, that Shakespeare, Tom Paine, even the great Faraday, all eschewed family life in favour of the bachelor's existence?

Still, his second wife, the limpid-eyed Mina Miller Edison, was impossible to refuse. As usual, she melted his devotion to his own thoughts, just as she had on the day he met her, in a feathered bonnet, during her inventor father's 1855 visit to present a contraption called a "motor-mower".

"What are you doing with a milk bottle, Deary?" she shouted, so that he could hear her.

He looked down. Was it still in his hand? Oh heck, and Cornaro in the other as well. He had been caught out. (She was greatly put out by his diet.)

She took the bottle off him, fairly snatching it. "Oh no, Thomas, enough!"

"Experimenting," he offered.

"Whatever for? And on a night like this? How many more turns of the century are you expecting to see?"

What a beauty she was! His best discovery, their love his most consoling invention, an incandescent thing, even – he would tell her with Shakespearean excess – a filament to span the oppos'd polarities of his soul, bringing forth radiance.

"I'm not sure yet," he replied. "Too many interruptions. How can I know? Can't git any damn work done."

"Come down as you are. Everyone's waiting. I said everyone's waiting. Come now." She stood her ground.

"In a minute."

"Come now."

"Soon."

"Right now. I'm serious, right now."

He was won over. He sighed as her gown washed down the staircase like a foaming tide. He tucked the book under his arm and reached blindly behind him to turn off his most famous invention. The bedroom fell as dark as history as he stumped down the stairs after her.

EDISON

1878

On the workbench a crude light bulb burned. The weak glow produced by it was as yet not strong enough to illumine the hilltop laboratory, but six gaslights made up for it, throwing light into the large workroom and onto the desk on which the inventor lay curled.

Alva. Thirty-two years old. A shabby Prince Albert coat. Deeply asleep after his three-day vigil watching over each new prototype of the electric lamp. And neither the phonographic recording, long since having finished playing an aria (cycling only static now), nor the several long *hoots* of the New York to Menlo Park could wake the exhausted genius.

"Mr Edison?"

A man in his mid-forties, clutching a bowler hat to his chest with one hand and a leather valise in the other, called from the doorway. "Sir?" Getting no response: "Mr…" *(louder)* "MR EDISON?!" When this shout failed to wake the man, he touched the inventor's shoulder with some concern.

Edison's eyes popped open. "Mary?"

Loudly: "Sir, forgive me."

Edison sat upright, yawning, stretching stiff limbs. "Eighty. Eighty decibels, no more."

The visitor, concerned: "SHOULD I SEND FOR A DOCTOR?"

"Eighty decibels. Not so loud."

"Apologies. Should I send for a doctor?"

But Edison needed no doctor. "Well? What is it? Who are you? Speak up. What time do you have?" He moved quickly to the working light bulb, the most successful lamp to date. He bent to it, inspecting its white-hot filament. "Yes my lovely…" Then, checking his fob watch: "Nearly two hours. You see?"

"Whitcomb Judson, sir. A great honour. I wrote to you."

Edison went to turn off his wax-barrel phonograph.

"I'm an inventor also," Judson announced with a proud smile. "The inventor of the – I'm still not quite sure what to call it really. You offered to view my invention. Give me your verdict."

Edison sighed. How tiresome fame was: an open invitation to re-duce to zero the physical space between the admirer and the object of admiration. Obligingly: "You have it with you?"

"Oh yes. In my pocket here."

Edison glanced at his fob watch once more. "Very well. Let's have it." At which, Judson handed him a rolled-up piece of fabric. "What does it purport to do?"

"It's, well, it gathers fabric. Fabric. It's a, well, an 'Automatic, Continuous Clothing-Closure Device'. That's one name I have for it. Though a touch long-winded. Perhaps a 'Clasp Locker' is more… You see, it aims to supplant buttons entirely, by – you just slide the channelling device upward you see, and like a, well, a plough in re-verse, it draws the divided tracks together."

Edison wearily tested it. "A reversing… plough? You've come to show me a reversing plough?"

"You're – oh" – disappointment showing – "it's um – you're one of my heroes, sir. My admiration is immeasurable. Like you I have no formal education. Just hard work, a clear head, the mettle to stay with a thing till it works. Imagine, inventing something that everyone needs, that will ease the intolerable burden of being alive!

Life is hard, so what better thing to do than to make life easier. Oh, sir. And then, to be remembered always for making the lives of others easier!"

"What's wrong with buttons?"

"Beg your pardon?"

"Buttons. What's wrong with buttons? Speak up. Your whole idea, and by the sound of it your whole life, is predicated on the fact that buttons need superseding. So what's wrong with buttons?"

Silence to this.

"I... I... well... if... I hadn't expected such a question."

"I can see some small utility for those with palsy, but... I wouldn't deem this a sizeable market, would you? I don't think you've got anything."

Judson's face fell – no, it collapsed. "Really? Nothing? Oh my. Oh my. I thought... I had such hopes. Such... h... hopes."

"Welcome to the inventing racket. You know how many of my 1,000 patents have turned a buck? In the end? How many have caught on? None."

"None? But, your – all these – your phonograph at least—"

A second visitor entered the room.

"Mr Edison."

When this man was neither heard nor noticed, Judson offered advice. "Eighty decibels." Taps his ear with a finger. "Louder."

"Mr Edison? I have some papers for you!"

Edison turned. "What is it?"

"Sheriff Taylor, Menlo Park! Pardon the intrusion, but I'm afraid I have to serve you with these here papers!"

"Papers?"

"Yessir! Due to unpaid loans these premises, this workshop, the farmland and all dwellings under your name are to be auctioned by order of the National Bank of Commerce!"

"My workshop?! My workshop?! Get out of here. Out!" He threw the papers back at the man.

The Sheriff, a pale round face but with fluid eyes, showed regret. "Sorry to bring such news. I hold you in the very highest esteem. Good day."

The Sheriff was gone, leaving the papers on the floor.

Edison turned to Judson. "Still want to be an inventor?" He kicked the papers under a workbench, his anger evident. "You don't make money from improving the world, you make it from its destruction."

"I… I had no idea," Judson said.

"Good day Mr—"

"Judson." Dejected, he prepared to leave.

"Look" – taking pity on the man, Edison reached out his hand. "Come back. Leave it with me, your whatever-you-call-it. Your plough. I'll – perhaps I'll turn it over in my head, who knows – it may have some other application far removed from the original purpose, which is often the case."

"Really? Then please keep it."

"Would you show yourself out?"

A train whistle blew loudly.

"You'd better hurry. The two-fifteen is leaving now. If you run—"

"Thank you. An honour. Thank you. Goodbye."

Alone, Edison sighed, inspected the working electric lamp again, then took out his fob watch, checked the time, picked up a pencil and entered the time in a logbook, as another train whistle was heard.

The smoke and steam from the newly arrived train fell from his shoulders like a cape, and stepping free of it the world's most famous banker came into daylight and drew from under his arm a copy of the *New York Times*, dated 21st December. With better visibility he was able to read again the headline: "Great Inventor's Triumph of the Electric Light", before he refolded the paper and set his silver-tipped mahogany cane on the warped boards, its crisp tap a telegraphic message to all within earshot that he was about to make his move and that the way should be cleared. He had come alone and in secret. The last thing he needed today was a fanfare. He intended this visit to Menlo Park to meet the great Thomas Alva Edison to be a complete surprise.

A station boy at Menlo saw the banker's face and retreated as if from a phantom. The ferocity of that expression was truly menacing, but how could this child with a broken broom know what Wall Street had to remind itself of daily: that this look of rage was the man's neutral face, his mood at zero, the norm. Such ferocity was merely the price you paid for holding the keys to the world's treasury.

And then there was his nose. No prominent figure in history had been lumbered with such a nose, not even Giovanni de' Medici, whose prodigious papal profile necessitated the Vatican's first rectangular coin. But J. Pierpont Morgan, the "Napoleon of Wall Street" – as *The Times* had christened him – was strangely pleased with his own disfigurement, and he would not swap it now for the prettiest nose in Christendom. It was as if to say, "I am extraordinary. And so I will look extraordinary."

As severe a case of rhinophyma as any doctor had ever seen, it had, over the last two years, mutated to twice its original size, and was now ivied with fine blue veins, a pustulated, bulbous magma of warty tissue with the texture of a cauliflower. Bizarre, revolting, upsetting to strangers, he carried it nonetheless with a kind of mad bravado. Cures were available and repeatedly offered, but he stubbornly refused to pursue them. But this did not mean he didn't care about how he looked. Not at all. He despised mirrors, and in their place he surrounded himself with a coterie of beautiful young men – men who served, in effect, as his reflection. It was no accident that the younger bankers at Drexel-Morgan were among the most handsome men in New York.

Furthermore, portrait artist after portrait artist – even the great Steichen – discovered the banker's true vanity when they were fired for paying too great a fidelity to their eye and too little to the complicated ego of their client. Newspaper editors fared no better, risking financial ruin if they failed to touch up their daguerreotypes, whiting out the true proportions of the colossal and grotesque appendage. Even the seemingly all-powerful "Bet-a-Million" Gates suddenly found himself barred from eighteen private Manhattan clubs of which Morgan was a member when he coined the nickname "Livernose" and when this jest echoed back to Morgan.

No, holding on to the nose as it was, turning his back on all possible cures, it had to do with its practical usefulness.

To decode the game J.P. Morgan was playing, you had first to understand that he was rich.

How rich? While there were some who doubted that he was the richest man on the planet – Vanderbilt, Carnegie and Rockefeller muddled this argument – all agreed that there was hardly any country that wasn't financially at his mercy. The world greeted him with a smile because it had to. And while he expected it of them, he also knew that the smiles were impure. Could he trust anybody? The classic rich man's problem. How to spot his friends among those grinning masks.

Here the divining rod of his nose came to the rescue. It never failed to elicit some response that was useful to him.

If in business, for instance, someone seeking a loan flinched or looked away at the sight of the nose, became nauseous or made a lame excuse to leave the room, then he would know at once that this person was a weak type, the pusillanimous sort to fall at the first emergency, and that therefore his chances of getting his money back were at risk.

On the romantic front, if a woman fainted, as many a fair lady of society had done at her first exposure to the nose – only to betray her husband in the next instant by agreeing to a secret rendezvous or permitting him on the balcony to embrace her from behind, his whiskers tickling the back of her neck – then he would be grateful to know right away of her concealed penchant for an ugly tycoon.

Lastly, if a lover ever mentioned his disfigurement with real affection, saying that she loved it, she adored it, even that it aroused her and made her cry sometimes after making love as though for a beloved pet that was unwell, then he would smell a rat at once and begin subtly to ditch her. He had no need of true love. His nose had saved him millions of dollars.

So how could he possibly regret owning it, or possibly consider treatments to cure it, when strangers were made transparent by it? Yes, *transparent*. That revolting, throbbing, sebaceous cauliflower gave him a psychic's insight into people's characters.

* * *

With his flaring top hat – brim size 7⅝ – and a monogrammed cigar smouldering between the first two fingers of his right hand, Morgan set off up the station platform with the high, looping gait of a man leaving a trampoline.

He tipped a Negro worker as he left the station, crossed Lincoln Highway and climbed two hundred feet of boardwalk towards the three-storey clapboard house. He stopped where the boardwalk gave way to a muddy track. A hundred yards higher up the hill sat the laboratory. He decided to start with the house.

He was met at the door by a Spanish servant, who immediately appeared to fall under his hypnotic control.

"J.P. Morgan, to see Mr Edison."

He had to repeat himself before the stunned maid came to life and hastily retreated.

The lady of the house, when she arrived, was at least able to muster some poise.

"Mr Morgan? Can it be? How extraordinary. How are you, sir? Welcome. I'm Mrs Edison, Mary Edison, sir."

This plain woman was in her dressing gown. This was a grave demerit at such an hour, but the banker let it go when she proved her character by looking no other place than in his eyes. He deduced from this a solid woman of high principles.

"Madam, it is so kind of you to tolerate such an intrusion. I am here on business unexpectedly. A surprise visit if you like."

Intrigued by the man's appearance – a velvet-collared coat, white kid gloves, stiff-winged collar, striped trousers and ascot – as well as by his natural grace and great height, Mary instructed the mesmerized maid to show the gentleman to the laboratory.

"Alva eats there with the boys… his staff. If he eats at all. We never see him when he's on to a new invention."

Morgan was pleased to hear this. "And how often is he on a new invention then?"

"Always," she said. "Without end."

The laboratory on the hilltop was a brand-new alley-shaped two-storey structure, a hundred feet by thirty. Mary showed Morgan inside, and before retiring pointed him towards the desk in the corner, where her husband, making notes in several books at once, had his head bowed, concentrating deeply.

Morgan crossed the room and announced himself. "Sir?" No response. "Sir?" But Edison continued to work. "My God, I heard you were deaf, but this is extraordinary. Oh, for pity's sake" – drubbing his cane loudly – "SIR!"

"One second," the inventor muttered, as a large shadow fell over his writing.

The banker shook his head in frustration and filled in the time by noting the details of the inventor's desk, five pigeonholes labelled: "Money", "Light", "Financial", "Amberola" and "New Things".

This last hole was choked with papers. Morgan then turned to observe, on a nearby shelf, several vitrines full of alcohol preserving in solution as many dead cats.

Edison rose. "Good, sorry about that. And who do we have here then?"

"Thank you. At last. How does anyone manage to do business with you?"

"Business?"

"Yes, have you heard of it?" At this point Morgan stepped closer to the lamp, presenting his face fully in the dim light.

Edison reacted with shock. "Morgan!" And then, upon seeing the famous nose at close range, in the flesh so to speak, added: "Oh my goodness…"

"I came to take a look around, sir."

"You… you take me by surp—" – Edison's eyes remained on the nose – "by… uh… by surprise."

"I would be bitterly disappointed if I did not."

"J.P. Morgan here! I hardly warrant it."

"For both our sakes it would of enormous benefit if you began to do so."

"Oh my Goodness. It's… it's… incredible… astonishing… completely without…"

"Without?"

"Precedent. I… I hardly credit it."

Morgan, keenly aware of the intense scrutiny of his nose, and of the inventor's half-completed orbit – Edison moving to look at his face from all angles as if it were some scientific phenomenon – narrowed his eyes, a look of absolute disgruntlement crossing his face. "Be careful, sir. Be careful what you say next. "

* * *

Though these two men had never met officially, it was possible that in recent months they had met twice, the first time by inadvertently taking a bath together.

After the trials and triumphs of that summer in 1879, and during the final push to perfect the lamp, the inventor had lost his ability to sleep. He had become a prisoner of catnaps. His stomach pains worsened and were impervious to analgesics. At the height of his powers and reputation he was in torment. The untimely death of his nephew, Charley, whom he had raised like a son but who had died enmeshed in a homosexual intrigue in Paris, had hit him hard. And so, gripped by whole new levels of guilt, and while his workers sought to improve the lamp without him, he heeded the advice of his principal collaborator, Charles Batchelor, and went with his wife to take the waters of Saratoga Springs.

A day after Edison and Mary had settled into their rooms at the Grand Union Hotel, and with his ailments aggravated by the bone-rattling journey, the entire resort was thrown into an uproar by the arrival of a mystery entourage.

Rumours spread: it was definitely the Morgans. A maid serving breakfast had made the first positive sighting. The nose had shocked her.

And then the hotel's blind masseur verified it: yes, it was definitely them.

So why was J. Pierpont Morgan in Saratoga? Was it he or was it his wife who was ill? Several theories arose, only to be displaced by even more hare-brained ones: the famous banker had had a physical collapse, a burst appendix, a herniated testicle. Others went further: he'd suffered a nervous breakdown and the news was being kept from the financial markets, lest they go into free fall.

The result was that the restaurant was full every night. The resort's entire guest list – predominantly Europeans, mostly women, many Jews – was hoping to see the party. Women looked out for Mrs Morgan, longing to copy her Paris chic, while men fantasized about trumping the banker at euchre in the private bar after supper.

Throughout the episode Edison remained calm, even if he was barely able to get any service while the banker exerted a magnetic pull on the resort staff. Edison's coffee when it arrived was cold, the toast stale, the waiters dismissive. Still, he resisted the idea that Morgan was behind it all.

Seated on the east veranda after an early-evening sun shower, the inventor thought he spotted a tall top hat in a swirl of female companions making its way through the garden topiaries. But he told himself it could be any wealthy satyr preying on the spa's many heiresses.

Then at dinner the waiters ferried trays of exquisite cuisine to an area cordoned off from the main restaurant, a room denied to prying eyes. It had to be the Morgans. The entire restaurant angled their seats towards the door, but Edison instructed Mary to hold her nerve.

And finally, slipping into a scorching spa the next afternoon, step by step entering the pool and opening his legs in the spuming waters, feeling his innards relax at once, he thought he saw, among the men playing dominoes on floating trays, the enigmatic gentleman himself: the hint of a deformed nose, the blazing eyes, just a few feet away.

But then the steam grew thick again. And when it next cleared, Edison found that the man had vanished. Had he imagined it? He put it down to the extreme humidity and got out at once, heading for the *piscine froide*.

It was out of hand, he complained to Mary. In a matter of days the spa had attained the hysterical atmosphere of that other famous spring: Lourdes.

Back in his room, Edison combed the *New York Post* in the hope of finding news that Morgan was in fact in Paris or Vienna, or that he had been spotted buying antiquities in the Valley of the Kings, thus proving that the resort sightings were simply a reflection of the public's obsession with wealth. Making money in itself was uninteresting, he told Mary, and "Morgan worship" had to be resisted. Fame should attend great public service. Statues should be erected to humanitarians, never profiteers. And in this regard he might have expected a little attention himself, at least *one* invitation to a cordoned room? Had he not long ago placed himself in the service of the public? And with his latest project, the lamp, was he not committed to easing the unbearable load of man?

If the phonograph craze had now died down – and yes, he admitted the queues for demonstrations outside his lab in Menlo Park had petered out – gone now the girls who fainted and had to be revived in side rooms with fans, faded the headlines "Orchestra in a Box!" and "A Machine that Talks!", vanished the daily articles listing his 158 other inventions – his success with the electric lamp had dubbed him wizard for time immemorial. What a great summer that should have been to be Thomas Alva Edison. Newspapers spreading his name to every corner of the globe. Children in Russia knowing it before those of foreign presidents. How the public had responded to his story when it broke internationally. A self-made man, a working-class hero – uneducated, even ordinary, but able to develop miraculous inventions through sheer hard work and brains. Take the April Fools' headline that many thought no joke: "Edison Invents Machine to Feed the Human Race – Manufacturing Biscuits, Meat, Vegetables and Wine out of Air, Water and Common Earth". Who was to say the inventor of an electric lamp was incapable of such a thing?

And yet, for all this public gratitude, even love – for in America he was a prophet of betterment – his fame had failed to translate into adequate room service at an off-season spa.

Alas – such is the eclipsing power of money. How he loathed these Wall Street types. The truth was that for all the public attention he had earned almost nothing from his inventions, and he held bankers and company men responsible. No sooner did his creations leave his laboratory than the patents were snapped up by their kind, to make money from, while his own small earnings had to be sunk back into the next endeavour, leaving him poor. His stomach was currently in knots about his inability even to settle the current hotel bill. He made a mental note to have a word with the maître d' – run off a provisional estimate of the total so far.

Mary closed her magazine and rose from her deckchair on the balcony. The medicinal waters were doing her no good. In fact her nerves, which had been giving her little peace since she had married Alva ten years earlier, were now appreciably worse every day. While his eccentricities might make good copy in the papers, they played havoc with her health. Forgoing her usual kiss on the top of his head, she went up to bed, shouting back to him that, in her opinion, he was simply jealous of Morgan. She added that she was ready to go home as soon as he was ready.

* * *

The inventor's second near-meeting with Morgan had been a month earlier at a valedictory banquet at Delmonico's in honour of Morgan's father's retirement from the world of transatlantic finance. Astonished to receive the invitation – never having had any dealings with the Morgans – he wired his RSVP.

Mary, feeling poorly, declined to go with him, and without anyone to tell him what was being said in the speeches he sat in silence at an inferior table in the packed room, oblivious to a rant by the Democratic presidential nominee, Governor Tilden, on the rise of American money and the decline of British influence.

Edison's chair, badly positioned, faced an immense sugar sculpture of muscular, American Stanley in Africa rescuing an effete, insipid Englishman, David Livingstone. The pro-American tableau was melting so fast in the heat that it was only a matter of time before Stanley (above) fell and crushed Livingstone (below), liquidating him altogether.

The sculpture allowed a small view – via a trapezoidal window defined by Livingstone's thigh and Stanley's melting musket – through which he could just glimpse Pierpont in a white tuxedo, tended by a fleet of waiters with trays of *timbales à la périgourdine* and partridge with truffles.

Taking an idea from an ample-bosomed woman who had forced open a French door to a balcony, he rose and went to take some air himself.

Stepping out onto the pillared terrace, he spotted a flash of white gown. The woman had gone to hide behind a potted shrub. Should he bother her? Was she waiting for someone? He inhaled the smell of lilac and philadelphus, then stepped closer, preparing a stilted introduction – "Madame, so sorry to interrupt..." – but found the lady being roughly kissed.

The lady's hands danced over her lover's neck and shoulders with enthusiasm, running through the wispy curls on the back of a bull-like neck, fighting not with disgust but with passion.

The inventor stepped back, ruing the scrape of his shoe which alerted the pair to his presence.

The woman opened her eyes, saw him, then froze, her bosom open already, her face crimson, her chest heaving, full of blood, while the man, protecting his identity, tightened his white tuxedo around him and, without a backward glance, stalked off down the terrace, heavy heels clacking on the flagstones, a cane materializing and striking the paving ahead of him.

Morgan! – it was clear to Edison then that he had just interrupted John Pierpont Morgan in an act of love.

* * *

Morgan's eyes were piercing, blue. They were two fearsome jewels in a big, doughy, Welsh head. But in those eyes – or perhaps more truly *around* them, as emotion and intelligence are dictated more by their setting – sat a fragility and loneliness that was in stark contrast to the grievances of his face. He smiled, and behind the Cyrano profile was a face of some pleasantness, a wide plain slashed with horizontal creases over the forehead, verticals from the nose to the sides of the moustache, between the eyebrows also, deep grooves born of years of scowling.

23

The two men squeezed hands.

"Remarkable," Edison said.

"What is so remarkable?"

"Well sir... that Mr John Pierpont Morgan is in my lab! And I can see now why you've come to see me."

"Oh? And why is that?"

"I do not wish to offend, but I presume that it's – it's your" – tapping his own nose – "that brings you here?"

"You presume wrong, sir."

"Then forgive me. I thought you must have heard about my work. In the field of electro-therapeutic forces. A whole new field I'm opening up single-handed."

"I heard no such thing."

"Then please accept my apologies. I'd presumed you'd come – seeking a cure. For your..."

"A cure? Not at all. But, had I come for that reason, what could you do for it?"

"I have several patents pending right now: an electric salt-water bath, an image-capture device to reveal the internal organs, a medicinal cabinet, calibrated for every disease, in which the patient sits... In this case... I think I would attach electrodes and run current through it at varying rates."

"A current? Through my nose?"

"Five ampere would do. To excite the particles, reinvigorate the tissue, reawaken cellular intelligence."

"Cellular—" Morgan touched his nose, almost protectively.

"Oh yes. Every cell possesses its own native intelligence. But this intelligence can go to sleep, prove harmful, causing maladies in the body. The blood stagnates and the entire organism is congested. Our spirits are affected, our moral fibre also. Criminality takes over, which is what an illness is... delinquent behaviour among cells. Actual criminals, for example, merely suffer from stagnant blood, a sleeping moral intelligence at a cellular level."

"But I am a banker, sir. Not a criminal."

"It would still be very interesting to try. Would it not?"

There was a pause, then Edison resumed. "So forgive me for staring, Mr Morgan. I was merely looking for a good place to attach the terminals."

The banker blinked. He shook his head. What could you make of such a man? "You astound me, sir. Astound me. You have a nerve. A nerve, I'll say that."

"These are astounding times."

Morgan nodded, finally ready to pay a tribute. "Clearly you are implicated in that."

"Yes. It's true, I'm doing several things in this laboratory right now that have been kept secret from humanity since the dawn of time."

Morgan recognized that the very sensationalism he had hoped to avoid was the only type of talk this man indulged in, and so he might as well get used to it. "I've come to see your inventions. All New York is abuzz, aglow, aglitter." He raised his voice: "YOUR INVENTIONS, SIR! I'VE COME TO TAKE A LOOK!"

"I see. And can I ask – which one? I have so many."

* * *

The laboratory was an exposition of the wonders of the world.

In addition to Edison's own miracles, the latest works of many rival inventors could also be seen. Advances in almost every field had found their way, in prototype, to Menlo Park, either to receive the maestro's sacred blessing before being put into service, or because the device was so exciting to Edison that he wanted to acquire it himself, improve it right away and so accelerate its evolution. Nothing irritated him more than a contemporary who took years, even decades, to nudge a product forward, while he knew in an instant what was wrong with it, then in an hour how to improve it and in a month how to set up its mass manufacture.

He couldn't help himself. He was an expansive talent, a Mozart of the machine shop, and more artistic in his own way than a hundred who sold paintings in Washington Square. And if he was seen by some fellow inventors as a pirate also, he could justify it. Why shouldn't he leapfrog another inventor when it was humanity who benefited? His wish was to provide the future *now*. At once! He had already vaulted technology forward forty years – according to the world's press – and if he kept at it then humanity could soon enjoy the fruits of the twenty-first century without having to endure the twentieth at all.

"Is it safe?" Morgan asked, closely examining the quality of soft light produced by the latest incandescent lamp. He raised his voice again: "I said, it's not going to explode is it?"

"Shouldn't think so."

Morgan was captivated, held his hand close, moved his fingers slowly, as interested by the shadow side of his hand as the illuminated obverse. "Well I'll be. You're a wizard, as sure as apples. Just like they say. Do you have any idea what you've done here? Do you?"

"I ought to. Made it from scratch. Been on it for two years now and pretty much got it worked out. Wanna get the bulb life up a bit, though. This one'll only run for somewhere on two hours. Every day we double that."

Morgan stared at the lamp now as if at something he had desired his entire life. "My, my, my…"

When Edison brought up the gaslights again, Morgan's eyes moved to a phonograph of radical design. "Fascinating. And what is this?"

"A tin-foil recording phonograph." Edison had Morgan lean forward, speak into the mouthpiece and then listen as the words were replayed – his own voice, preserved! Asking for a second turn, Morgan bent forward again and – determined to be more creative than during his first effort (nine repetitions of "*Hello*") – recited a short passage by heart from the *Aeneid*.

Edison played it back, to the banker's great delight, and then changed the roll, whereupon another voice came to life. "Madame Bernhardt."

"Really?" gasped Morgan. "Sarah?"

"Yes. She visited last week on her way back to Paris. She made this recording for me."

"What a gadget!" Morgan listened with relish to the histrionics of the world's most famous actress, recognizing the speech from Victor Hugo's *Ruy Blas*. "An extraordinary woman," Morgan sighed. "You know, I shook her hand once, last year after her performance of *Phèdre*. And while talking afterwards we discovered, she and I, that as small children we had both shaken the wizened old hand of Madame George, who had once been the mistress of Napoleon. And it struck us both that we could be one handshake removed from Napoleon. Then Madame Bernhardt pointed out that three or four such handshakes would form a chain back to Shakespeare. How very young the human story still is. Remarkable." He reshaped his moustache. "Look at it this way: from the bard's quill to… to a *talking machine*… in just four handshakes! And now… what's this?" Morgan had found something new to fascinate him.

"Oh. That? It's… an alternative to, uh… buttons."

"An alternative to buttons? Can there be such a thing? Show me. Show me at once. I *abhor* buttons! How wonderful! How does it work?"

ANTHONY McCARTEN

"It – you just draw the fastener up, and it draws together – still rather crudely – a poor prototype – it would need to be worked up—"

"Let me, let me. So you – just..."

Morgan worked the slider. His eyes grew large. "That is... one of the most... beautiful things... I have ever seen." Up and down he worked the slider. "Look at that! It's like... a plough in reverse. I want it."

"You want it?"

"The rights to it. Are they sold?"

"No, I... I need first to... to refine it. Need to rename it too. Something more... zippy. But I have, uh... high hopes for it."

"Imagine, a world without buttons!"

Edison shrugged. "Buttons are indeed a tyranny... one from which humanity must eventually be released."

"Perhaps we can do a deal? For both items."

"Both?"

"Yes, this, and your lamp, your incandescent lamp."

"My lamp?"

The lamp in question, at that very moment, gave out: *pop*!

* * *

Edison led the banker on a full walking tour of his complex, the first research-and-development facility the world had seen. In glass reliquaries sat many more highlights – as well as several low points – of the inventor's career: the stock-ticker (still used on Wall Street, the flow of prices being punched onto paper tape), the electric pen (its point a needle to perforate holes and make a stencil for multiple copies of a document), a perfumed plastic rose for buttonholes (in prototype only), a refillable cigar (ditto), the quadruplex telegraph (able to handle four messages at once over the same wire), the water telephone (a farce), ink for the blind (a concept), artificial silk, the inductorium (a wooden box in which he'd fleetingly believed he'd discovered the forces behind occultism) and the loony Tasimeter, which had failed abysmally in its attempt to measure the sun's corona during an eclipse, but whose regulator he'd adapted for use in the lamp.

They stopped at the sole work of Edison's nephew, Charley, at sixteen a great talent, who by himself had improved Bell's telephone.

"Far better than Bell's. I sent him to London, to present it to the Royal Society. He fell ill. Died. My nephew was the second-best inventor in the world. Even *I* can hear a caller on it, so that's a pretty darn good machine." Edison grinned.

"How much *can* you hear?" Morgan asked loudly.

"Enough – too much most of the time. Most of what we have to listen to is rubbish."

Morgan took the question seriously. "What about the words... I love you? What if you can't hear these?"

"Yes, but how many times have you heard them?"

This shocked Morgan. He faltered. His anger rose again. "I can answer that. Twice. My mother, when I was twelve. I'd been particularly charming. And a young woman, on a bridge, once."

"Your wife?"

"Don't be ridiculous."

They came to something new: an invention covered with a black cloth.

"What is this one?" Morgan asked.

"It's... well, based on the recording phonograph you've just witnessed. One day I hope to... it's a dream of mine... to... to make a machine sensitive enough to capture and record... human memory."

"Memory?" Again Morgan's eyebrows rose. "How so?"

"My work suggests that memory is released at the point of death into the ether and is swarming all around us all the time. With a sensitive enough device we might even mechanically reclaim the voices of the dead in the same way. Your lady on the bridge perhaps."

Morgan looked worried. "Be careful," he said. "Be very careful with that one." And with this Morgan was invited to dinner.

* * *

As an Edison phonograph played a recording of a Strauss waltz, the party of five sat at dinner. The two Edison children were in high spirits. With their father back at the head of the table after many days' absence, and with their bedridden mother in a fine, red-velvet gown featuring a stuffed bird at the shoulder, they couldn't suppress a game of pat-a-cake.

Edison was, as ever, immune to loud noise – since boyhood he'd lived in the near-silent chamber of old age. It was left to Mary to send the nine-year-old Marion and the six-year-old Tom junior away to the kitchen to eat with the maid, so their father and Mr Morgan could talk.

"Dot!" Mary barked. "Take your brother. Dash, leave your sister alone. To the kitchen, at once."

This joke, first made over their cribs, naming the infants after the telegraphic language of their courtship, had stuck. "Mr Morgan will think we have taken in a couple of Indians."

Morgan smiled, but soon looked relieved when a more adult atmosphere settled on the dining room.

"How did you enjoy your tour?" Mary asked.

"So many wonders on show," Morgan replied brightly. "History in the making. Mrs Edison, what do you make of the incandescent lamp?"

"I like it." Sensing more was expected of her, she added: "I hope it may one day prove extremely useful."

"Indeed."

The inventor was more wistful. "It is easy enough to invent things to set the newspapers talking and make people gasp, women faint. The big trouble comes when you try to perfect your inventions, to get them to market."

"Perhaps this is where I can assist you."

As Edison and Mary exchanged a quick look, Morgan rubbed his hands together. "Your husband's lamp interests me."

"Why?" Mary asked.

"Why? Well, for one reason, because diamonds look dull by gaslight. I'm sure Mrs Edison understands this." He wasn't joking either. "It's a great complaint of the ladies. At dinner parties we always revert to candlelight. I am an aesthete, Mr Edison."

Edison *had* heard. Who had not? Every year the papers documented Morgan's trips to Europe, reporting that he was looting it of art with the professed aim of making it unnecessary for an American to travel there at all. And he had been very successful. If the churlish British still denied him the Elgin Marbles, a Gutenberg Bible was his, as were Napoleon's watch, Shakespeare's first folios, Catherine the Great's snuffbox, the coins of eleven of the twelve Caesars (a Marcus Aurelius still eluded him), Leonardo's notebooks, jewellery belonging to the Medici family, paintings galore and statues to fit out ten museums.

"But not everyone wears diamonds, Mr Morgan." The humanist spirit of Tom Paine was alive in Edison still.

Morgan smiled with surprising warmth. "Oh, I'm sure more pedestrian justifications can be found for your lamp." He then groomed with thumb and forefinger the twin sable brushes of his eyebrows.

"You're too late," Edison said. "Vanderbilt already bought the American rights."

"Yes. But what's he doing with them? I'll tell you what. Nothing. The old man's dying – and the son, William, is a wobbling bowl of pea-juice jelly. The old man infantilized the boy. You don't want your rights with Billy when the old man pops off."

Edison was shocked. He'd imagined these two barons would be close friends. But then, perhaps they were.

"Let me be blunt. Mrs Edison, if I may?" Mary nodded. "Let me help you illuminate Europe."

"Illuminate…"

"Europe?" Mary gasped.

"From the Caspian to the English Channel. Light it with your electric lamp. Streets, houses, offices. I'll arrange the finance. What do you say? Agreed?"

"Agreed?" Edison had to laugh. "Agreed? I don't think you understand."

"Understand what?"

"I haven't lit up a single house yet!"

"But you will. I presume. With you it's only a matter of time. So let's start with Europe as soon as possible, and then see how we do. First a triumph abroad, then let's see if I can't talk with Vanderbilt about lighting New York – and then the rest of America. What do you say?"

What a character! Edison thought. A man for whom the unfeasible was the only challenge worth undertaking.

Morgan continued: "I have a vision of my own, you see."

"Evidently," Mary interjected.

"Of a better world. May I explain? Of a superior one to the difficult, gruelling one we all presently endure, this wretchedness, day in and day out." He poured himself some more wine. "Please, excuse my philosophizing, but I have such a good feeling today. I suspect it's your fine food, Mrs Edison, but – for some time now, almost ten years, I've had a vision, of a simpler society. Where bankers play a larger role. A system devoid of warring greedy small companies, always duplicating the services of near-rivals, indulging in ruinous competition. *Inefficiency*. That's our great enemy today. Inefficiencies in the market, brought on by rampant competition. Nobody benefits from this competition. Least of all the poor, the workers, the men and women who toil and suffer. So I propose… *combinations*. Single large companies. A new model! Run by professionals, men of honour, with knowledge of money, who can curb human greed. Have you noticed that in times of great greed it is always the poor who suffer? Bankers, efficient large companies, can change this. No government meddling in everything. You see? Efficiency goes up, costs go down, the public benefits. Combinations! I tell you! Holdings extending, extending beyond national boundaries, liberating mankind, delivering on the broken promises of our founding fathers."

The silence which followed this also accompanied the service, by two handsome Negresses, of quartered pheasants.

Mary asked: "More potatoes?"

What a human being this is. Edison shook his head in awe as he beheld someone who had everything that it was possible for a man to have, but who still wanted more. More complex than himself, a noted philanderer in his private life (they said he had footed the bill for a hospital wing in New York to carry out his girlfriends' abortions – but, at the same time, had also become, just this week past, the sponsor of a nationwide campaign to cover over the genitalia on America's nude statues), this national enigma, a living contradiction of values, was now in full flow.

"Potatoes?" Morgan replied. "My figure is already too memorable. Thank you, but no. Now, where was I? Anyway, for ten long years I've been coming to this point, awaiting a new industry to come along, one that can be built afresh, one based on a product so essential that everyone will have to reach into their pockets and buy into it. And I have a hunch, sir, such a wonderful premonition, that your little lamp there could be that product. So. What do you say? A marriage of science and banking. Your vision and mine. A marriage majestical."

Edison stared at this man, this phenomenon. "I had always believed competition a good thing, the lifeblood of originality."

"Heavens no. I'm not sure you heard everything I just said."

Mary replied: "Oh, he heard. I've been tapping on his knee."

"His knee? I don't understand."

"In Morse. Morse Code. We met in a telegraph office. Where I worked. We are both experts."

Morgan looked delighted with this. He leant towards Mary, smiling broadly.

"What a wonderful system for a husband and wife to have. When you can't get through to the other side, you just send them a wire! Ha! Ha!"

Mary smiled. Edison did not.

"Have you wired him that yet? Ha! Ha!"

"Not yet. Perhaps later."

"Ha! Ha! Priceless. Priceless people!" He then folded his napkin and rose. "Water closet?"

"Oh. Yes. Down the hall," Mary pointed. "Third door."

Morgan exited. The noise of his shoes faded away.

Mary, leaning close to Alva's ear, said: "He scares me, Popsy."

When her husband failed to react, deep in reflection, she tapped these words in Morse on the tabletop.

Edison watched the tapping hand. When the hand fell still, he said: "Yes, he scares me too. But what else can we do? And Europe. Europe! And all our debts. Our home. My workshop."

Mary's hand did not wire a response.

"But you're right," Edison continued, thinking aloud. "He's a crook. We'll be fine… And yet, what we could achieve… My God. In the Civil War he sold the US Army guns that were actually the property of the Army already. Did you know? A huge scandal. I swear, Popsy, I have such a fear of these bankers. Developed it early, a deep concern over the look of ownership that crosses their eyes as the cheques are signed, the false friendships, the inevitable invitation to dinner, the fourth glass of wine and what I'd do or promise or say, the 'understandings' that would be reached around midnight and, at last, the whittling-away of my independence and creativity and freedom – until I see, from a rosy distance and over that last glass of brandy, the loss of myself."

With the growing sounds from the hall of Morgan's return, Mary composed herself, checking her lipstick in the reflection on her silver knife.

THOMAS

1929

Thomas opened his eyes. Where was he? Had he been sleeping? No, it was some old-age approximation of sleep. He had merely been recalling days past, his head resting against the window of the private railway car, his straw hat pushed askew on his head. He sat up, straightened the hat and saw that he was in fact alone in the ceremonial car.

He had been left in peace to gather his strength for the day ahead. How he dreaded the events lying in wait for him farther up the line at Dearborn, where a crowd of four hundred would already be assembling! After all these years, his arrival would be the highlight of the day. His many "admirers" would be there, the giants of the business world. How deeply these people wished to show their appreciation on this golden jubilee of his greatest invention! Walter Chrysler was coming, Harvey Firestone and Ford himself, the principal architect of the celebration. Orville Wright also, Charles Schwab from Wall Street. J.P. Morgan Jr would represent his late father. George Eastman loitered in a bowler hat unadorned by a ribbon. Harmed by her discoveries, Marie Curie got feebly out of a car driven by Nelson Rockefeller. Albert Einstein stood by in Chicago, ready to send a message by wireless. A cable was expected from Hindenburg.

Ford had even moved Thomas's very first New Jersey workshop to the jubilee site in Dearborn. Bricks had been numbered, hauled six hundred miles across country and reassembled in order. And

President Hoover was waiting for the train two miles out of town, ready to jump on board like a hobo and ride with Edison the last few miles into town. Even presidents wanted to be at the old man's side when this train made its finely planned arrival.

But the train was stopping. Why? Were they in Dearborn already? Lifting the blind, Thomas saw no pennants and streamers outside, no festive crowds, no presidential party. Instead he recognized Walker's Cross, a forgotten siding on the Grand Trunk line. With its dilapidated platform, servicing a dwindling community of swineherds living in tornado-battered clapboards, it was evident to Thomas that Ford, finding himself ahead of schedule, had decided to lay up here awhile in order to kill some time.

* * *

At a speed the world had largely forgotten, the ceremonial train came to a steaming stop.

The weather was oppressive, sticky, breezeless, hot: even the jackdaws, hunched on the wireless telegraph poles, looked shiny with sweat as the conductor encouraged the travellers to stretch their legs on the platform. Excited talk broke out as they stepped from their rich carriages out onto the warped boards amid the dissipating steam.

What a sight the old place was! Not for years had this siding even justified a telegraph operator, let alone a station master, but with the arrival of women in fine lace and peacock plume, and men in formal black talking of great affairs, the old place was flung back sixty years to its heyday, when the local racecourse had drawn in punters from Kalamazoo and ice creams were sold by boys in pleated shirts all along the platform.

But alone in his darkened car, the famous inventor couldn't be encouraged to leave the train. He was left to rest, the blinds drawn down. His energy was limited, and he would need all of it to get through the celebrations ahead. There was some concern that he'd taken a turn for the worse today. A few even said that the old boy might have seen his last sunset.

Although nobody could be certain about how close to death he was, it was well known that in his eighty-third year his ailments were so multitudinous that it was implausible he could ever fully recover.

"He's got Bright's disease now," one female invitee whispered while taking a small grey pill herself before passing the water bottle to her son. The group around her shook their heads in anticipatory sadness, then added the names of other illnesses known to be afflicting him: "Diabetes as well, I heard. To add to his woes."

"Kidney malfunction, they say."

"Is it any wonder? I *mean*! Two years now and he takes in no other food than milk. A slow form of suicide if you ask me."

"Milk is all he'll touch. I heard that. Got constipation and malnutrition bad now too."

"Really? I heard stomach ulcers and uraemia."

"Oh, he's had those *for ever*."

"Good Heavens," added a pastor. "It's a miracle he's able to draw breath, let alone work."

"Is he working?"

"Oh yes. They say yes. Most certainly. Still at work. On a machine to... well, it's not to be spread about... but he's trying to invent a device to" – he stepped closer to his listener – "allow us to speak with the dead." There was no look of irony at all in the pastor's face.

"*Really*? Will that really soon be possible?"

"In this day and age, who is to say not?"

"Ye gods. Well, I fear we'll all be using it to speak with him soon enough."

At the same time as predicting Edison's last exit from worldly affairs, each of them knew that a man who had spent his life in the business of surprising the world could never be entirely counted out. This living legend had that veneer of indestructibility which old elephants acquire, and it still wasn't outside the realms of the imaginable that the rumours of imminent death might yet prove to be the work of minds too paltry to digest miracles.

On the platform, standing guard over his darkened ceremonial carriage, and with her back to its window, Mina Miller Edison – "lovely" was the word that came readily to most people's minds when they spoke of the inventor's wife of forty-three years – received the spoken tributes of his friends on his behalf. "Thank you," she replied gently, and "thank you so very much," and then, "he would be pleased to know this," she told all the gentlemen and great ladies, shaking every hand, smiling benignly, dipping her head in small bows in a prayer-like way. At the same time, with her left hand behind her back, she stealthily relayed in glove-soft Morse on the side of the railcar every compliment back to her husband inside. She knew that even if he was napping he would still feel the vibrations of her secret transmission and be able to decipher every word.

"A great man," she secretly wired.

"Irreplaceable…"

"A rarer spirit never did steer humanity…"

Tap-tap-t-t-tap. Tap-tap…

Next, a Southerner approached her, a naturalist who had forsaken a safari in Kenya to come here today to observe another endangered species. He shook her hand. "He has promised to live for ever. Well, we'll darn well hold him to that."

Next, a gentleman of the Boston press. "Madam, we have progressed more in the last sixty years, thanks largely to your husband, than we have in the last 4,000."

"So kind, so kind," she said, as she made the sheet metal at her back vibrate like the membrane of the inner ear.

When this man had gone, Mina received at last a telegraphic response. A single knuckle tapped on the glass sent by her husband. Slowly but surely he gave her his summary response. When she decoded it, she gave her lunar smile.

"NO MORE. HAVE MERCY. STOP."

As usual, Mina was keeping an eye on him. She guarded and watched over him. Without sleep for days in the lead-up to this event, she was suffering too. But how did he respond? By teasing her. Mercilessly. Still, she loved him, and understood his outer limitations. His soul, with which she was in communication, was in good shape. Her beloved Thomas, this world figure, technology's ringmaster for more than sixty years, he loved her on wavelengths not publicly detectable. But these were all completely readable by her. Looking after his reputation for decade upon decade, still correcting his old friends when they called him Alva (his boyhood name, which she erased when she turned him publicly into Tom, so much more solidly American to her ears), she protected that three-part name as she protected his corporeal self: with long-learnt patience. And if he responded by playing with her emotions, telling her constantly that he was at death's door, so what? By preparing her for the end, she knew what was codified into these actions too. These days, whenever she said she was popping out to the store, he told her beforehand: "Kiss me before you go, when you come back I'll be gone."

"Stop playing, Thomas. Seriously. Please don't say such things."

"Oh, my bird, I wish I was playing."

But she knew what he was telling her with such quips. And so, of all the family, she was the least troubled by them. She had already made the necessary inner preparations, was listening out for his deeper signals, and was certain that when the old boy was finally ready to make his move she would know it, and be ready.

"REST IN PEACE," she quietly tapped in ironic reply before moving away from the carriage to dispense courteous smiles to the next celebrity to shake her hand.

* * *

The guests reacted to the conductor's whistle and re-boarded the train, and in the flurry that followed, nobody noticed the last-minute flight from the guard's wagon of a ghost in a black-serge suit, a flat-topped straw hat, white wisps of hair behind his ears. As the train drew away, the figure steadied himself with a cane, and only when the train had gone up the track did the steam waft away and reveal him.

The inventor looked around him. What had he done? What act of folly had he just committed? Well, it was too late to stop the train now. And as the smoke traipsed away, the facts were as they were: the principal object of the day's festivities, the man at the centre of this unprecedented tribute, had just escaped his fans in favour of an empty railway platform. What had got into him? He barely understood it himself. He took a deep breath and looked about, feeling pangs of stupidity and guilt. Weak in the legs he reset his cane, filled his baggy lungs to capacity and then made for a wooden bench by the station door, some thirty-odd paces away.

How long before his people on board realized he was gone? How long did he have?

He knew that Mina would stand guard over his darkened car until the last moment, letting him sleep, keeping the public at bay as usual. Close to Dearborn, at the last minute, she would go into the private car to wake him, only to find a note in his place, the two-word message he had left for her.

Reading his genuine "I'm sorry" – because he cared only about upsetting her, he rated her higher than presidents – she would guess his foolishness right away, just as she would recognize the deeper meanings behind the crazy escape act. Then she would sound the alarm. The engine would screech to a stop, and after a few minutes of metallic chaos slowly reel in the miles back to Walker's Cross, albeit going faster in reverse than it had moved forward all day. *An hour then,* he deduced. *An hour at most,* to sort through all his troubled, pressing memories, fifty years of old scores which had driven him off the ceremonial train, and which, if not dealt with here and now would render him incapable of facing any of his old friends this day. How perverse, he thought, how extremely odd, that a collective display of love should drive him to such depths!

Sitting on the forgotten bench he cursed again his decision to permit this day to go ahead at all, a day that he should have known would bring such junk to the surface. For a moment he even revived an old idea to revolutionize the calendar, as the French had done after the fall of the Bastille, purging it of all celebrations and traditions – but he let this go. The old man pondered: fifty years since the invention of the electric lamp. Fifty since that day. Fifty! But in that time – what? His most secret dreams and his most mysterious projects were still only prototypes in his head. The inventions that would finally lift humanity out of its morass, where were they? He had had some fun with the cinemascope for a bit, but others had taken that forward, made it their own. He had actually been in professional decline for half a century, while his regrets only grew stronger, more aggravating, as time went by. Why had this been so?

He knew the answer of course. The first years after his invention of the electric light bulb had nearly ruined him. He had emerged from them in tatters. Damaged internally. And it had taken a long time to recover. He understood as well as anyone why our gravest mistakes give us more and more trouble as time passes, not less. For while it is true to say that one usually errs whilst under some sort of unusual pressure, whether internal or external, it's also certain that in the months and years that follow the incident, the first thing to fade is the memory of those pressures, so that the mistake soon stands alone in memory: crude, unjustified, inexplicable, out of character, exposed like a wreck by a receding tide. And so out of character do these aged mistakes eventually come to seem that we are often left wondering if our gravest errors are not in fact the work of some impostor.

So it was today. The great Edison of yesteryear was gone, the pressures forgotten, leaving only the pale old figure to answer for the mistakes of a younger man. Did he even have the strength left to own up to those mistakes afresh, and so finally make amends in his heart, begin to understand them before it was too late? In fifty years of trying he had not managed it. How much less likely it was now, now that the steam had almost gone out of him?

Before he went deep into his memories, he tried to take stock. First things first: where the hell was he in this present moment? If he couldn't answer that question, then he wasn't going to get very far with all the others he needed answers to.

He took air, looked about him at the destroyed station. Entropy was the law of all things, and he had known Walker's Cross from a flying visit over fifty years earlier. It had been bustling with life back then. Now he saw only a single busted-out wooden building bounded by scorched barrens stretching towards the dusty horizon. A few words by Longfellow came back to him:

> *Waste are those pleasant farms, and the farmers forever departed!*
> *Scattered like dust and leaves, when the mighty blasts of October*
> *Seize them, and whirl them aloft, and sprinkle them far o'er the ocean.*
> *Naught but tradition remains of the beautiful village of Grand-Pré...*

Waste! Decay! Like his own body, the shoebox station house had all but collapsed. Below, on the tracks, the sleepers were splitting in the dry heat. The telegraph poles stretching away east and west were as haggard as lightning trees. How could fifty years do so much damage? Any day now the same October winds would blow for him too, and lift high his own particles, scatter them o'er the ocean. Therefore, he had to hurry. His time was short. He had a heavy mental itinerary today. Much work to do. He settled back, closed his eyes and began to sift his past for the crucial minerals. Amongst the rubble and sand, kernels of gold. This day to remember had become a day for remembering. Thus he began his heavy labour, starting with a list, a remembered list: of all the people he had ever killed.

EDISON

1878

"Mr Edson? Mr Edson!"

At the end of the long wooden pier, itself at the edge of his Menlo Park property, Edison fished, lifting and lowering his line. He turned. "Tesla. What is it?"

"I haff something to show you." Nikola Tesla, tall, wiry as Paganini, late twenties.

"Not now."

"You will wish to see."

"Not now, man."

"You will wish to see, Mr Edson."

"Are you hard of hearing, boy?"

"No. My hearing very good. Thank you."

At that moment Edison felt a twitch on his line. "Huh! Felt something then." Tesla waited patiently. "Well, what is it?"

"I am now making a great discovery."

"Aren't you supposed to be working on improving efficiency in our new dynamos?"

"This is more important. I haff uncovered the secret of the sun."

"What are you talking about?"

"A motor and a generator. That works – on alternating current. AC."

"AC is dangerous."

47

"Not now. I haff tamed nature. All the time everyone say this alternating current cannot work. Only direct current – your current Mr Edson. But AC is the natural current produced in a dynamo, so how can nature be bad? No, they say, 'uncontrollable'. It is bad, dangerous, must be converted to DC."

"I'm trying to fish."

"In Austria they laugh at me. In Paris laugh. In London laugh. But now I build my machine for you, Mr Edson. Because you – you are a man not fearing the future. Like me, your mind is open." Another twitch, and then Edison felt a fish take the hook and run with it. "I don't believe it."

"But it's true."

"I got one. I had no bait on my hook. What do we do? Here, you do it."

"I?"

"You. You. You."

Tesla stepped forward, took over and started to reel the fish in saying, "Steady, steady, OK, OK, here he comes, oh my beauty, here he… see him? Look at him! It's biblical! Biblical! Pass me the… quick—" Edison passed him the net. "Look at this! Here we go." With a tug a large catfish is on the dock, flapping, gasping, thrashing about for life. "Hit it!" the Serb instructed. "Go on. Hit it. Hit it. Give it a knock. On the head. Hit it hard. A short sharp shock."

But Edison couldn't bear to hit the fish. "You do it. Here—" He pulled a wooden mallet from the pail and held it out. "Take it."

"I pulled it in," Tesla protested.

"Here. You. Please."

"What's the matter?"

"I don't want to. This is a new shirt."

Tesla sighed and dropped the rod. "Give!" Taking the mallet he struck the fish hard. "There." But then – another spasm of life in the fish. Tesla bashed it again – even harder. Edison winced – he didn't enjoy watching this, and even averted his eyes. "There." Tesla said, sure the fish was now dead, until the fish started to flap once more. Tesla struck again, struck hard, but a second later another flap from the fish required an even mightier clubbing of the head. Tesla was wincing now. "There." But still his work was not done. Seven, eight, nine more heavy blows were needed until the fish lay still, and by then great flecks of blood marked Tesla's shirt and face.

"Oh," Edison groaned.

Tesla dropped the mallet, breathless, and began to cough.

"There's… some blood. On your face." Edison took out a hand-kerchief, began to wipe blood off his employee's cheeks.

"So," Tesla asked, "not interested? No. You are interested. With my current you can light the world, cheap, safe."

Edison stuffed the handkerchief in Tesla's hand. "Go back to work."

"Not interested?"

"No, I'm not. Get out of here."

"SIR!"

"EIGHTY DECIBELS, MAN!"

"HOW CAN YOU NOT BE OF INTEREST?"

"EIGHTY DECIBELS! Are you deaf? There is no point in pursuing that current. I've tried it. It's a dead end."

"For you. Not for me. Tesla will take his payment, and his invention, and go elsewhere. Please to pay me my fifty thousand dollars."

"What?"

"Fifty thousand dollars. You promise me. I redesign two dozen of your direct-current dynamos. I work eighteen-hour days. Replace, replace, improve. I shall haff my money. You must pay Nikola Tesla now."

"I have no money to give you. Do you understand? There is no money."

"You haff money. In the newspapers they say—"

"Gone."

"You have stocks."

"Worthless."

"You haff cheated."

"I owe you a great deal. You did good work on those dynamos. So let's find something else for you. We will work this out. I need men like you."

"But Tesla does not need men like you."

Tesla kicked the bloody fish back into the water, stormed off, leaving Edison to watch smaller fish move in to feed on the sudden bounty.

* * *

Edison found his wife in bed as usual. She was in a depressed state, reading a book on theosophy as she ate chocolate after chocolate.

Heavily pregnant, swollen to three times her normal size, she ate only chocolate now, upwards of a pound a day. Once, when he had criticized her diet, she had gone to his library and found a justification for it in one of his own dietary textbooks. Arming herself with the theory by an Italian nutcase that the body could exist on a solitary source of nourishment, she was now expanding this experiment to see whether it could apply to the heart as well. In this endeavour she would be just as resolute as her husband.

Edison knew when he was being criticized. She blamed him for all her troubles. But he rejected this, refused to have this accursed act of martyrdom on his conscience, along with everything else. "You can't just survive on any one thing alone, Mary." He was appalled by the idea. "The body needs diversity," he told her. "Cornaro in his book didn't mean it literally. The cells need variety. Variety, Mary.

Meat. Vegetables. You'll kill yourself and take the new baby along with you." Silhouetted in the doorway, he shook his head in helpless dismay, then picked up a cowrie shell on the dresser, pressed it to his ear. Unable to hear the sea, he put it down again. "Brace up Mary, for God's sake. Brace up. And git out of bed. Doctor Lehman says this is more than half your trouble."

"Get up for what, my dear?" she replied to his face, and then again to his back as he left the room. "For what?"

He moved to her side on the edge of the bed, and only then did she see he held a pen and a document. "And you have to sign this, Popsy. The lawyers said that if I put everything in your name the sheriff might drop the auction."

"There's something wrong with me, Alva! In my head. I'm so awfully sick. My head is nearly splitting and my throat is so sore."

"Just sign. I don't know what else to do. Come on, sign, sign, just take the pen and sign it, SIGN IT POPSY!... sign."

But instead of taking the pen she began to sing, mournfully:

> "I am an 'elpless female, an unprotected female,
> my husband's been and gone.
> I'm left alone to sing."

"Sorry," Edison interjected.

> "...My Popsy Wopsy's vanished from my sight,
> and we might have been so happy so we might."

Copious tears filled her eyes. Edison touched her cheek. "I've been caught up. But from now on I'm free. Why don't you book us a holiday?"

"No."

Moving away, he began to take off his shirt. It was late. Perhaps he should try to sleep in his marital bed for once. "We'll take the waters at Saratoga Springs."

"Saratoga Springs?"

Mention of the waters never failed to cheer her. "There you go."

"Can we afford it?"

"No."

She picked up the document and pen left at her bedside and signed it. She then drew back the covers. "There. Now. Come to bed."

He came to her, kissed her on the forehead, stroked her face tenderly, but did not get in beside her. "Soon. I just need to send a telegram."

"Can it wait?"

"Not this one. Ten minutes. Promise."

Wearing only his underwear, he hurried out of the room and into his private study. He turned on the telegraph transmitter and began to tap.

DEAR SIR STOP REVIEWED YOUR OFFER STOP HAPPY TO PROCEED ALONG LINES DISCUSSED STOP TA EDISON

THOMAS

The long-necked boy was no more than sixteen and had every right to be surprised to see the only bench at Walker's Cross station half-occupied by a white-haired ghost wearing a suit and hat from the previous century.

The boy marched forward and sat down, avoiding looks sideways, aware only that the old man emitted a strong odour of chewing tobacco.

In silence they waited, neither moving, until the old man sighed, coughed, winced, staunched the fit with a stout rap of fist and then drew from his pocket a small mandarin. The old man peeled the fruit and set a single segment in his mouth. At first the boy avoided the insult of staring, but when the old man's chews – accentuated by the clicking of his jaw – increased in number, passing twenty, thirty, then forty, he couldn't resist a sideways glance. A second piece of fruit was being mouthed, a tiny morsel which actually didn't need to be chewed at all.

The old man swallowed, sighed, then turned. "How old are ya?"

The question, coming from nowhere, surprised the boy. "Ah... old? Old? Ah. Fifteen, sir."

"Louder."

"Fifteen, sir."

"Louder."

"FIFTEEN."

"Too loud. Eighty decibels. Don't shout." The old man nodded nostalgically. "Fifteen? So, got a job, Mr Fifteen?"

"A job, sir? No sir."

"What the hell's wrong with you?"

"Sir?"

"You're a man now."

"I help my father on the farm, sir."

"Git out from under, son."

"I will, sir."

"It's a big world out there now." The old man's gaze seemed to be just then perceiving it. "It's been opened right up. Ready for you to walk right on in."

"Sir, I know."

"Right on in. Lot of old men opened it right up for you."

"Yes, I will."

"Make sure you do."

"Thanks."

"Just make sure you do no deals with the Devil."

"THE DEVIL?"

"Too loud. Eighty decibels I said." The old man muttered something unintelligible before reaching up to brush dandruff off his shoulders. After a deep intake of breath, a deep expulsion. The wind blew hot and humid across the barrens.

"What's your name? Seeing we're both stuck here."

"Winthrop, sir."

"Winthrop, you say?"

"Yes sir."

"So… Winthrop, where you going today?"

"East, sir."

"East, you say?"

"Yes sir. Is that the train you're waiting for too?"

"East? No. I'm waiting on a different train from that. Mine… well mine's gonna be a strange one indeed. Gonna be going in reverse."

"In reverse?"

"'s right."

"But we don't get 'em coming through here in reverse, sir. Never do."

"Just you wait 'n' see."

"No trains through here go in reverse, not ever."

"Well. We'll see about that. Silver dollar says I'm right. How about it?"

The boy deliberated. "Silver dollar? No sir, haven't got that much to be throwing away on no train going in reverse."

The old man nodded approvingly. "Good for you. Gambling is for fools. Hear what I say, son?"

"Yes sir."

"Who is gambling for?"

"Fools, sir!" the boy shouted.

"And where ya going?"

"New York."

"New York, you say?"

"Yes sir."

"And why you going to New York?"

"Want to be a millionaire, sir."

"A *what*?"

"Millionaire, sir."

"Saints alive. I'm sitting here next to J.P. Morgan!"

The boy smiled. This old man was a classic of his kind: just as the very old should be: scatterbrained, straight-talking, full of unfathomable experience, unpredictable, inadvertently hilarious and shocking. "Millionaires sprouting up like corn ears in New York, so I hear. So that's where I wanna wind up."

"So that's where you going now? To Wall Street to make a million dollars?"

The boy laughed at the idea. "Yes sir. You bet. Like Mr Ford, Mr Firestone, Mr Rockefeller. You bet."

"And what are you prepared to do to get it, Winthrop?"

"Whatever I got to."

The old man nodded, but not agreeably. "Then you'll probably get it."

The boy brightened. "You think so?"

"You've got the attitude right anyhow." He sighed. "But a word of warning. Make a living. Fine. Make a million. Fine. Good luck to you, just don't make a religion out of it."

"Yes sir."

"I got close to doing that. Turned me upside down way back in the Eighties." He shook his head, turning over heavy thoughts. "Upside down. See, what I now know that I didn't then is that something electrical happens in the brain. There's a science to what happens when you give yourself over to a business way of thinking. A part of the brain gits bypassed eventually, out of disuse, rusts up, and that part is the regulator. The brain's moral regulator, the memory, is left out of it."

"The memory?"

"Read some Faraday. And don't make a religion out of business. Or you'll start seeing ordinary folk as something you can drain like an oil field, cut down like a forest. I was there when that style of thinking took a-hold of Wall Street. Big Business they call it now in the journals, well I was there at the beginning when it started to get really big. Started with the railways, the main trunk lines, but it went wild with electricity. And the only error I'm making here is one of understatement. Folks had seen nothing like the scale of greed that spread out in the Sixties and Seventies. Yessir, I saw small business take a back seat in America ever since."

"Yes sir."

"Institutions came of age then that we got no hope of reeling in now. Bigger than forests, deeper than oil wells. Life of their own."

"Gee," the boy said, as the big face turned once more towards him.

"Now tell me... what don't you make a religion out of?"

"Business, sir."

The old man's face darkened even further. "Darn right. And while you're at it don't make a religion out of anything. Nothing. Especially not religion. Hear what I say? You want something to believe in, look at nature." He raised his cane, aimed its bullet tip at the surrounding hills. "There's your Supreme Intelligence. There's all the Bible you need. Take a look. You see a battle raging out there 'tween good and evil? 'Tween God and Satan? Bunkum. No creeds needed out there. Nature is Religion with the volume turned down." At that moment he unexpectedly jolted the base of his stick back into his solar plexus with the force of a gun recoil, but it did not suppress a raking cough. The stick fell onto the boards. The steam went out of him. His shoulders slumped. That big, Dutch-descended, sculptured head became unsupportable, a burden, falling forward.

57

EDISON

MY DEAR SIR STOP RECEIVED YOUR WIRE TODAY STOP DELIGHTED YOU HAVE SEEN FIT TO REVIEW MY MARRIAGE PROPOSAL IN A DIFFERENT LIGHT STOP ACCORDINGLY I SHALL ENDEAVOUR TO ARRANGE A MEETING WITH YOU AS MY FIRST PRIORITY UPON RETURN TO NEW YORK STOP REGARDS JPM

Morgan, aboard the SS *Britannic*, still at anchor at Liverpool, rechecked the return message to Edison with the ship's purser and then dictated a quick wire to his wife. The ship was about to depart and the ship-to-shore cable would soon be down.

MY DEAR SIRESS STOP TIS A MOST LONELY PASSAGE I AM ABOUT TO UNDERTAKE ONCE AGAIN WITHOUT YOU STOP FITS OF BLACK MOODS STOP WOULD JUMP OVERBOARD BUT FOR YOU AND LITTLE JACK AND FEAR OF CATCHING DISMAL COLD STOP DISCONSOLATE JPM

He then went to his cabin and loosed his collar, exposing before the mirror a necklace of lovebites.

For two days he did not appear. But then on the evening of the third he put on a heavy coat and made for the forward deck.

Hardly had he filled his lungs with frosty air than the alarm sounded. He heard the first mate cry out in the darkness "Hard a port! Hard a port!" – and the ship's engines swung into reverse. Water churned.

Morgan gripped the handrail for dear life. Then from out of the mist loomed an iceberg. A hundred feet ahead, as green as an emerald. The ship veered. But it couldn't entirely avoid it. The bows quaked. The rails shaved the pack ice. Morgan backed into the gangway as an avalanche of snow thudded onto the upper decks, tufts powdering the shoulders of his Siberian coat, settling on his moustache. He was alarmed, breathless, but excited also. His heart had begun to pump as it seemed almost to have forgotten how to do.

The crowds from the dining room then emerged – "Did you see?" "What was it?" – but the iceberg was gone already, lost to the mists.

"My darling, are you all right?!"

A voluptuous, diamond-clad beauty was by his side, her shoulders naked and goose-pimpled in the cold air. She took Pierpont's arm and kissed his cheek twice – it was a rash act. Morgan was careful to avoid such associations in public. Receiving a sterner look than any she had ever received in her entire life, the woman withdrew her arm.

"An iceberg," he said, his mood becoming sour once again. "That's all. Nothing to bother us. Now I'm going for a brandy. Alone. Come to my room if you like, later."

The woman nodded, backed away, threaded her arm into that of an elderly woman throttled by a mink stole and disappeared into the receding crowd.

In the piano bar Morgan played solitaire in a corner table and smoked a black Cuban cigar. His fierce expression warded off any who might have presumed he was in need of company. The cards did not fall well. His depression returned.

Just spared certain death, lost in icy waters, he was safe in the company of a society beauty, so why, he wondered, was he not happy? It was inexplicable. For all his efforts – turmoil, philanthropy, dedication to his principles, occasional relaxation of his principles – he seldom was simply happy. He was a deal-maker without rival and yet, in this most fundamental contract, he had been cheated. As usual, he dealt with such moods by drinking more than his doctors advised.

About 11 p.m. he felt the ship's engines stall, then stop altogether. The ship would lie at anchor for the night. The mist was too dangerous. He made his way to his cabin.

A perfumed note was taped to the door. This further indiscretion annoyed him. He tore it down and gave it only a cursory glance: its tone of desperation disgusted him. He went inside and locked the door.

He awoke with the sun.

He drew the curtains. A startling sight: a giant iceberg, two hundred feet from the ship's prow, as strange as an asteroid.

He went directly for a late breakfast, as arranged. It was his only official appointment of the crossing, and the real reason he had made the voyage in the first place.

The restaurant was brimming with chatter about the iceberg and how near they had all come to a watery grave. "Did you see it up close?" said one. "We wouldn't have stood an iceberg's chance in hell of surviving!" A devout Catholic simply cast her eyes heavenwards and made the sign of the Cross, while the Captain diverted the talk to the weather in New York.

Billy Vanderbilt was waiting at a superior table.

Morgan smiled. "Sorry I'm late, Billy. Did you see that iceberg?"

"Slept right through it all. I took a draught, y'see, for my nerves, and only awoke a half-hour ago."

"No, I'm not talking about last night's iceberg," Morgan said. "I mean the one out there now. Have you seen it? We're lucky to be alive."

"Oh, that! Quite beautiful isn't it. Like a fabulous cut diamond." A waiter arrived. "Give me the... the eggs... boiled... no... scrambled... oh I don' know... I suppose the Scottish gammon as well...

no, forget that… diet… and coffee… pot of coffee… and perhaps, yes, wait… a grapefruit, no, forget the grapefruit."

In no time Morgan ordered the grapefruit and a strong coffee. "Mighty sorry to have heard about your father."

"Thank you Pierpont. He died peacefully at least. But a man like that, such a figure, you feel they are almost incapable of dying. And when they do you simply don't know what to do next. The burden of his decision-making falls to you. You ask yourself at every turn: what would *he* do? What would he *do*? But of course my mind is nothing like his, so… I'm left unable to act in any affair with any confidence."

William Henry Vanderbilt, this tub of a fellow, struggling even to order his own breakfast, was indeed nothing like the man his father had been. Cornelius had been a titan, a white-whiskered rogue, a pioneer and empire-builder raging at his foes volcanically, chasing his chambermaids until the very end. But Billy, at fifty-five, was half-formed, neither of one mind or another, a flip-flop of indecision. Suddenly, like an explosion, the biggest inheritance in the world, estimated at $100 million, was his, and it terrified him. Fleeing so much power, William had taken to sea. His current stratagem was to cross and recross the Atlantic for as long as he could, avoiding all the responsibilities that would descend the second he set foot on dry land. During this period the business world was in ferment: to them it was an outrage that this mega-fortune had fallen into the hands of a near-imbecile. Under such circumstances, Pierpont had been dispatched. With Wall Street's backing he had booked a return passage, with the solemn intention of forcing on the Vanderbilt heir an abdication.

"Billy. Can we discuss the railroad?"

"Oh, not business right away. Surely."

"The New York Central Line. Time to sell, Billy."

"Don't you at least want to wait for your coffee?"

"It will only take a minute, Billy."

It was true. A minute was all that would be necessary for Vanderbilt to give Morgan the yes or no upon which Wall Street waited so breathlessly: one minute to decide the fate of a vast rail network that the late Commodore had so painstakingly built up over forty years, fighting off the Indians, feuding with his business rivals in a long, expensive war of attrition.

"Now, I know as well as anyone that a railroad is the most burdensome business there is. But I'm here to help you out, Billy, if you wish it."

"I fully expected you would have a plan."

"I try not to disappoint."

"Then make it quick, for goodness' sake." The richest man in the world tried to smile. But his laugh lines were shallow. Only the worry creases went deep. Overweight, homely, his hair glossy with shellac, he awaited nervously the banker's proposal.

Morgan spoke. He wanted the New York Central line. It ran 4,500 miles, in all directions from New York City and Albany to the Great Lakes and Chicago. It was Billy's and his alone now: the last great American line owned by a single family. The Commodore had run it from a cigar box of records, old style, but America was in a state of flux: even the Rothschilds were a fading force, having thought America would amount to nothing, backing Europe instead. Now the baronial age was drawing to a close. The bankers were moving in, eyeing the great fiefdoms, turning them into public companies, floating them on the stock exchange, transferring power from the old figureheads to mostly anonymous shareholders, keeping only the great surnames intact for use as letterheads. Now the last hereditary aristocrat in America was about to be asked to surrender his place in history.

Vanderbilt should sell. In a nutshell, this was Morgan's message. Without question he should rid himself of the railway lines this very day. What good were they to him? So much trouble! Morgan personally could take them off his hands, the New York Central line most importantly, handle the whole deal, take it public, perhaps even sell all the shares discreetly in England so as not to incite a panic. "Jay Gould might even take some, if I play it right," he said, adding that Billy shouldn't be alarmed at the inclusion of his father's arch-enemy in the deal. Feuds helped nobody, least of all the stockholders. Morgan offered to take care of it all, and for his trouble he asked only to be in control of the board. This would further steady the market when the news broke.

And what would William get, in return? Cash. A vast amount. Morgan scrawled the actual figure on a napkin. Billy took it up, read it. His face showed no change in expression. It was true. What need did he have for a business empire that would drain his last drop of blood? Money was useful, added to which Billy had no practical use for power. Morgan was quick to add that Billy was doing the right thing. Running a giant company was a form of self-torture. He related his own story. Night terrors. Bouts of ill health. Recurring depression. But Billy had the chance to escape all this. The sea-bound life need never end, if he so wished. Life was to be enjoyed. Yes, enjoyed. Not a crazy idea. "Have some fun! Get your health back. *Mens sana in corpore sano*." Morgan even recommended that Billy use some of the dough to buy up the land opposite his own new brownstone on Madison. "The whole block is going for a song. Be my neighbour. Could be a nice little investment. Think about it." Such a prospect lightened William's mood for a second – he forced a smile as he consulted again the napkin – but only for a second. The figure scrawled with India ink was no great comfort. His worries were broader and deeper than cash.

Their breakfast arrived and was set before them.

"And may I say," Morgan continued, "before we set business aside and enjoy our breakfast together – just you and I, like old times – that as the son of a great man myself I'd shudder to think you should suffer any shame or harbour a single dark thought that you were somehow letting your father down by agreeing to any of this. I tell you, Billy, and I tell you honestly, the shift from family to public ownership is a global inevitability, and the Commodore... well, he was never one to ignore the writing on the wall." Morgan picked up his spoon, inserted it into the grapefruit and prized loose a teardrop of pulp. "And the writing is not only written on the wall, it's engraved there already."

Billy Vanderbilt couldn't touch a morsel on his plate. Instead he stared at the yellow omelette, its garnish of parsley, the curl of fast-melting butter. Had he just agreed to Morgan's plan or not? Of course he had. And without uttering a single word. Before him now, instead of the burdens of office, lay an endless voyage: was that all that was left for him to aspire to? The weight that had been hanging over him since the old man's death was gone, but what was now to occupy him on this earth? Trifles alone? A state of tranquil melancholy? The slow depletion of a huge sum of money? His face registered the first signs of self-loathing.

Morgan put his hand on the man's shoulder.

"You've done the right thing. Your father would be proud. And now, if you still have the patience for it," Morgan resumed, "I'd like for just one second to touch on the small matter of your US rights in the Edison Electric Light."

"The electric light? You want that too?"

"Actually, yes. Surely you don't want it? Have you the patience to discuss this? I've given you an awful lot to digest."

"Patience?" William Henry Vanderbilt said. "I suppose that is all my life will now require. Just that. Patience."

* * *

Coming down the gangplank at New York harbour, Morgan saluted like a conquering hero.

"Are you all right, Pierpont?" his business partner asked once they had boarded the carriage headed directly for Wall Street.

"I envy Vanderbilt actually."

"Why so?"

"Did you see him disembarking before me? He's lost an empire, that man, one of the great empires, but he looks… well, if not happy, at least ten years younger, while I – I the victor – feel like death itself. What does that teach you about our profession?"

Hours later, his work done, Morgan returned home to his new brownstone on Madison Avenue, feeling spent and agitated. A black funk still hung over him.

He took supper with his wife Fanny, drank too much and spoke of his Atlantic crossing in weary tones, mentioning for her interest only that Billy Vanderbilt seemed to have put on a little more weight and that his own head cold, which had threatened mid-Atlantic, had fizzled out. She made courteous replies. Thereafter, the only sound during their meal was that of cutlery chiming on bone china.

At 9 p.m. she kissed him on the forehead. She was tired. She went up the flying staircase to bed – a dour, sad figure taking the steps on the tips of her toes. From the lobby he watched his second wife climb: as mother of his four children he respected her, but there was no illusion of romance between them, and little talk of fidelity. Marrying Fanny – doing so within months of the death of his first wife, the much adored Amelia Sturges – he had sought and found in Fanny a distraction from a traumatizing pain that would see him keep two dozen blooms on Amelia's grave all year round. Fanny, for all her virtues, could hardly compete with a first wife dying only four months into a young man's married life when happiness was at its zenith, when good luck seemed a certainty and passion indefatigable. Amelia was thus frozen in time, at her most sublime, with her beauty incandescent and perennial, while Fanny was allowed to grow old, heavy in the legs, broad across the rump, cold and dim in her attitude. And yet Morgan would never divorce her. As in business, having once made up his mind to trust someone – man, woman or child – he trusted implicitly, trusted until they failed him, and sometimes even *after* they failed him.

Morgan stopped watching her, crossed the marble flagstones, then locked himself in his study, where, not many moments later, servants could hear low moans coming from inside and, soon after, the sound of a man weeping.

* * *

The black-hulled, 185-foot *Corsair*, a floating pageant from stern to bowsprit, could also run as a steamer – and today, with no itinerary and with Morgan at the helm, it chuffed some way out into New York harbour before the motor was cut and five crew members went at the sails.

"I should pick up one of these myself," Edison shouted across the cockpit. He was wearing an absurd captain's cap with twin embroidered anchors above the peak, on his feet a pair of white shoes.

The banker smiled. "I'll get you into the club."

Edison looked up into the inflated sails. "So how much would a yacht such as this cost me?"

"If you have to ask, you can't afford it."

Edison laughed. But not as loudly as Morgan. The banker was enjoying his millions today, and happy to defy his father's axiom – that a banker's money should never be on display lest his clients wonder at whose expense it has been acquired.

Making better use of the breeze on the port side was a small, twelve-foot sloop, whose single sailor raised his cap in a gesture of good sportsmanship as he tried to overtake the grand vessel.

"Not today!" Morgan hailed. "He wants us to concede! Like hell. Very well then, we'll tack first."

And with a sudden heave of the wheel the *Corsair* came about. The crew was entirely caught off guard and very nearly tumbled overboard as the boom swung hard across. Morgan was shouting again: "Well, if he wants a race he can have one!"

The giant boat all but stopped for a few moments until the sails ballooned again and pulled the massive hull forward. The two vessels were now on a collision course, and as they crossed, the unyielding *Corsair* was narrowly in front. As its wake washed over the small boat, almost capsizing it, the solo sailor raised his arm in anger before pointing away, his sail going limp.

Morgan's eyes sparkled, and he called to the boys: "Get ready to go about again! I mean to teach this fellow a lesson in match-racing!"

Edison was astonished. There was so much clear water to be had and no need at all for a conflict here. But the crew were already hoisting a larger foresail. The inventor looked back over his shoulder for the little sloop which, keeping its former course, sailed away on the opposite tack to the Corsair, and no doubt away from danger. To Edison's untrained eye it appeared only a matter of time, however, before this lighter, quicker craft would turn and cross far in advance of the banker's lumbering, floating giant.

"Stand by to tack again! Let's go after him and keep him well covered!" Morgan shot a look at Edison. "He's fast... light... but we have the higher position, you see?" Morgan's gaze shot up at his own sails, which he kept full. This love of the fight, it had kept his bank's coffers brimming while America's fortunes rose and fell. "Quite a sport, isn't it?"

For the sake of politeness the inventor nodded.

"Now tell me, while we go after him, how do you feel about our little venture now? Oh! Before I forget. A change of plan. I talked with Vanderbilt, the son. America is ours."

"How?!"

"I took his railroads public. The old families – Vanderbilts, Rothschilds – are finished. So let's light New York properly! I'm taking you on, Alva. I'm making you my pet project. But I want you close by. Move into town. You'll be my right hand." Edison found himself nodding. "And tell no one. The first rule of engagement – never let the other fellow know what you are up to." And as if to underline Morgan's Law, he wrenched the helm without warning his crew. "ABOUT!" he bellowed, but too late: his crew were on their backsides, struggling to climb back to their feet on the angled deck and frantically pulling in the jib sheets.

Steadying himself by a handrail, Edison looked westward and saw that the sloop was coming back towards them. "Will he be all right? That man there. We were real close last time. And it's such a small boat."

"He can always concede – but you see, he comes back at me. He spoils for a fight. The human animal is crude – a fighter, even when the odds are impossible."

This time the sloop had an even better claim to right of way, having made good progress, but Morgan held a nail-biting line which, at the crossover, sent the little boat tossing in a swell that all but swamped it.

"Got him again!" Morgan gave a yelp of pure pleasure. "Got him! Ha! Ha! Ha! Did you see how it works? If you're upwind, stay upwind. Oh – more news for you. You're being sued."

"Sued?!"

"In London. Joseph Swan. He's saying publicly now he invented the lamp first. Claims he did it an entire year before you. Has all the proof in the world. Is it true?"

"I don't deny he invented a bulb."

"The first? Then we have a problem."

"But not a particularly good one. That's the difference. It wasn't viable."

"We have a problem."

"You see, my filament – my spiral filament—"

Morgan raised a hand. "Forget about all that. I talked to him in London. I wanna combine with him. How does 'Swannison' sound to you?"

"Swannison?"

"Yes."

"You want me to... get together with—"

"Combine!" – the voice, shouted above the westerly, above the roar of hull and ocean, was itself a roar.

"Combine with... someone... with whom I am at profound odds?"

"That's who you do combine with – those with whom you are at profound odds. 'Edswan' just didn't... Anyway, I've drawn up the papers. It's going to be sooo agreeable to have you in town, devoted to business enterprise alone. Leave inventing aside for now."

Edison seemed temporarily in shock. "For how long?"

"Oh, not long. A public demonstration, that's what I'd like you to think about. Convince the public that electricity is safe. A magnificent display."

"Well, a display of some sort was – was one of the things I was—"

"Capital! A party. You're upwind of me! Well, hold your course, Alva. Don't be swayed by anyone. Cheers!"

* * *

Hurrying back home to Menlo Park, Edison found Mary once more in bed. Beside her now, in place of chocolates, bottles of bromide took up the entire table. He sat on his side of the bed, panting hard from the steep climb up the hill from the station. In his right hand, a letter. "Mary? I came at once."

"Alva."

"Doctor Lehman. I just got his letter."

"What does he say?"

"'Your wife… is nervous and despondent and thinks that she will never recover.' Is that true, Popsy? 'And yet I can find no fixed reason for her ailments.'" He skipped a large section, then resumed: "'I believe that an entire change must be found at once… if Mary… is ever to…'" But he refused to read the final lines aloud. "Look, come with me to New York. We'll set up house there. A change, that's what you need. Morgan wants us to move there."

"New York? I'm… New York? I'm not strong enough to travel. And the children, their schooling. And my headaches are getting so bad. What's happening to me? I'm scared."

"Mary… please… listen…"

When she turned away he resorted to tapping in Morse on the foot of her bed.

Finally she responded. "I know it's only two hours by train but… you don't understand. I'm not myself…"

"Then… I'll just… if you're too weak I'll…"

About to capitulate to his wife, he heard Morgan's roar in his ear once more, extolling him, telling him that the world needs him now. The world!

"Look, just a few more weeks. Hold on. You'll be all right till then, won't you? Then I'll take you to Saratoga Springs. Let me just sort

71

our troubles. I have an exhibition to mount, a grand parade, and I'm lighting Morgan's house. He wants his to be the first house in the world to be wired for electric light. Isn't that something? To be the first?"

"I'll stay here. How long will it take? How long will it all take?"

He did not reply. All he could tell her for certain is that he will make it up to her. "I promise."

"And remember," she told him. "Remember, Alva, who you are."

"See, that's why I need you! That part of me that's liable to go astray, needs your daily messages. You're my own true Western Union." A kiss on her forehead, gentle, prolonged. "Saratoga Springs. Soon. I promise."

* * *

Nine paces were sufficient to take the inventor from the bookcase to his desk, where he opened again the letter marked "Private":

Your wife indeed seems very nervous and despondent and thinks that she will never recover. And yet I can find no fixed reason for her ailments, other than what Dr Beard calls in his new book "American Nervousness". In it he identifies several new factors in society injurious to our well-being, such as too many new ideas introduced too rapidly, excessive commercial activity, the repression of emotion as well as interior confinement, such as is now occurring in the workplace and at home. These contribute to what he calls an "anxiety habit". At any rate, I believe that an entire change would be of benefit to Mary in order to...

Edison put down the letter and scribbled a reply.

Dear Doctor Ward, thank you for your informative letter. As it happens I have just decided to take my wife off on a trip very soon. Thank you for your thoughts on American anxiety. I suffer from this myself. Consider this – perhaps I have infected her. I hope not, but I too suffer from some strange inner turmoil (felt mainly in my stomach) which I fear has no entry in your almanac, and which began with the invention of my electric lamp. Since then it has defied my own cures. You speak of the dangers in exposure to too many new things. How is an inventor ever to be well, in that case? As for Mary, might she simply be allergic to me? Are there such cases? Yours, anxiously, T.A.E.

Setting down his pencil, he lay on the couch. He had only just decided to turn himself into a businessman, but already an internal turmoil was taking place, a modern nervousness.

He got off the couch, which was too soft, and lay on the hard floor, staring at the ceiling. He closed his eyes and tried to sleep.

* * *

Until that moment the Columbus Day parade down Madison Avenue had been a procession of tried-and-true crowd pleasers: clowns, costumed serfs, mock conquistadors, three galleons – the *Nina*, *Pinta* and *Santa Maria*, their paper sails billowing – and a fat Columbus on his poop deck, his spyglass aimed at a cluster of Hasidic Jews.

Families applauded and laughed from behind the cordons. But the happy shouts died away to silence and even to fear as the Edison Electric Light Company's new promotional exhibit rounded the corner.

At first, parents covered their children's eyes. There were screams. Women put hands to their mouths. Men peeled off their bowler hats in slow motion. What was this? Were they witnessing a catastrophe?

ANTHONY McCARTEN

Marching in box formation and at cortège pace, two hundred uniformed men came up Fifth Avenue like an invasion force. This would have been disturbing enough, had not the head of each man been on fire.

But not quite on fire. The flame was contained by glass – imprisoned in a flask, an upside-down pear, affixed to the top of each man's derby. Golden-headed, ablaze, each marcher a human lighthouse, this moving mixture of flesh, blood and torch drew gasps as the public realized that the fire-bearers were in no particular pain. The youngsters giggled and screamed with delight as the excitement infected the adults, who finally began to talk, then chuckle, then laugh. Oh, that wicked man, that unsurpassable wizard, Thomas Alva Edison – he'd done it again: he had turned people into light bulbs.

At the second-floor window of a brokerage house, sweltering in the heat, J.P. Morgan lowered the field glasses, which had been trained not so much on the parade as on the reactions of the public. Electricity, believed by so many to be a killer (even a liquid, as one newspaper had held, lethal when it leaks into soft furnishings), was shown to be so safe that one could channel it through one's very person with all safety. The banker stroked his moustache, nodded agreeably, making in his head a daily forecast of profit, then began to dictate to an attractive young woman behind him a message:

MY DEAR SIR STOP A FAR BETTER EFFORT STOP YOU ARE SHAPING UP NICELY STOP AN OMEN OF BETTER THINGS TO COME STOP I PREDICT NO SMALL IMPROVEMENT IN STOCK VALUES TOMORROW STOP LET US NOW SET ASIDE THE WIRING OF MEN FOR THE TIME BEING STOP WIRE UP A HOUSE NEXT STOP I OFFER MY OWN STOP LET US NOW PROVE TO THE PUBLIC THE DESIRABILITY OF YOUR SYSTEM FOR DOMESTIC EMANCIPATION FROM DARKNESS STOP IN FAITH JPM

* * *

The disruption to the Morgans' social life by Edison's men and machinery was considerable, but Pierpont was so fascinated by the electrification of his Madison Avenue mansion – the first domestic reticulation of electrical current ever attempted – that he didn't move out during the great upheaval.

In between cataloguing his growing collection of books, illuminated manuscripts and chromolithographs, he smoked his huge cigars and regularly came out of his study to watch workers feed wires through the existing gas lamps, fix bulbs in place of camphor wicks, pull up the floorboards. The future! He was watching the future unfold first-hand. And how thrilling it was. He even descended stairs and climbed ladders to watch the men root around in the basement and in the ceilings.

All social luncheons and dinners were suspended.

Mrs Morgan, resigned to this army occupation but far from fascinated, kept to her rooms, insisting that the gas fixtures be left alone. She was no fan of experimentation – not of any kind, whether human or mechanical.

And, eventually, the work was complete. Carpets were rolled back in place, paintings re-hung, the wainscoting retouched, tulips set again in the recessed inglenooks below the all-new electric lights.

"It's done," Edison told the relieved Morgans.

"Truly?" Mrs Morgan asked.

"Shall I show you how it works?"

* * *

A week later, on New Year's Eve, the first guests to the Morgan Mansion in a month came up the path and were struck at once by the shrill screams of awe, amazement and consternation coming from inside. At the door, Mrs Vanderbilt, a little tight with champagne, shouted, "Wonderful! Here comes another victim! Oh goody! Let them through!" Room was made for the arriving guest, all eyes lowered as the newcomer's shoe alighted on the first step. The crowd hooted as the shoe's pressure made the house number on the door light up. Then, on the second step, and by the same sorcery, the doorbell rang all by itself, and on the third, the door swung wide open to reveal Messrs Morgan, Drexyl and Co., waiting for the new guest with a flute of champagne, a fat cigar for the gentleman – lit by touching its end to a glowing spiral on the wall – and a dazzling hostess ready to lead the party into the ballroom.

"Welcome to the twentieth century," Morgan declared with a deep chuckle. "Come inside. There's plenty more in store for you. Why not start by having your shoes shined electrically?"

A second pool of people was gathered in the lounge lit by a hundred bulbs set in the former gas-light fittings. There, coffee could be ordered from an electric urn. Visitors could watch toast being grilled electrically. The ceiling was a planetarium of glittering lifelike stars and, on opposing walls, one moon rose as if by levitation, as another set.

In the centre of the room a game, quite like musical chairs, was in progress: here men in top hats, multimillionaires mostly, giggled as they dashed between one of seven armchairs, each one eliciting an astonishing response to the weight of each thrill-seeker. One chair caused a hidden piano to start playing, another set off a sewing machine. Another lit up a gaslight. Drums started playing. A great bell rang in the ceiling and then stopped. The guests were in a lather.

Edison arrived late, but everything was running smoothly. Morgan went beyond his normal handshake and embraced the man; then, taking him by the arm, presented him as the equal of the best in the room. Fuelled by champagne served by waiters from Delmonico's, bowties were soon loosened and women danced to phonograph music with men other than their husbands.

"So when is the new power station going to start up?" William Vanderbilt asked Edison.

"Soon. Very soon."

The tycoon smoothed with one hand his black, side-parted hair and made his hostility plain. "It's a wonder Morgan has any money left with the speed he is pushing you."

"The speed *I* am pushing myself, you mean. But he has shown great faith in this product, yes."

"Judging by tonight that faith has not been misplaced. You must wire up my house next. Will you? The Vanderbilts are a family of progressives, you know. Come and see me next week, will you?"

Billy slid back into the glittering crowd as Morgan advanced. "You don't have a glass, Alva. Come, drink. A great day for civilization."

On the stroke of twelve, a life-sized effigy of Jupiter raised a glass to its mouth all on its own. As its nose glowed, it then addressed the crowd by way of a phonograph mounted inside it.

"Happy New Year!"

Pledges of vast monies were whispered into Morgan's ears, only to be doubled in the next instant, as he herded the revellers out onto the front lawn to sing 'Auld Lang Syne' and watch a cannon mounted in the chimney electrically send fireworks into the sky over Manhattan. The impression of a flawless future was sure to remain in the minds of these people for the rest of their lives.

* * *

Four days later, Morgan's house was surrounded by fire trucks. The rooms inside were poisoned with the smell of burnt wood and scorched carpets.

Morgan stood at the giant front door of Circassian walnut in a silk bathrobe to meet Edison, his jet eyes retaining something of the just-quelled flames. A newspaper was gripped under his right arm and he aggressively led the inventor under the unbroken stained-glass dome in the reception hall and up the stairs to the private study, where the fire had been most intense.

Servants had already stacked smoke-damaged treasures in the middle of that room. Glass reliquaries had protected the most exquisite items, but many antique books lay smouldering on the floor.

Morgan's face was graven, and his nose throbbed redder than usual. Even now sparks fizzed in the converted gas fixtures. "What have you to say? I put my faith in you. Not to mention a great deal of my money."

"I'm sorry. Do you want me to remove the system?"

"It's my wife's wish that you do so at once. But my wish, now that I have sunken several millions into this folly, is to see if we can keep this a secret."

"Of course."

"Publicity like this would destroy us with the veracity of, well, this fire." He tossed a blackened book onto the sooty heap. "It would confirm everyone's worst fears about electricity."

Edison looked around him. He saw the extent of the tragedy. "The wall coverings survived."

"Yes. Silk damask. From the palazzo of Agostino Chigi, fifteenth century."

"Thank God the ceiling."

"Fifteenth also. From a Venetian villa. Shipped in one piece."

"I will ensure it doesn't happen again."

Morgan fixed the inventor with a glacial stare.

Later, over a lunch of duck *à l'orange* hosted by the silent and unmoving Mrs Morgan (who seemed to be locked now into a perpetual sitting for a portrait), the inventor heard Morgan's full list of complaints.

Edison sprinkled water on a napkin and tamped his brow. The humidity and heat in the house, caused by the new coal-powered generator below them, which gulped one ton of coal a day, were still extraordinary. Edison was baking. He promised to set India Rubber supports under the entire house. He vouched that this would dampen the vibrations caused by the generator, which Mrs Morgan described as "apocalyptic" and which, she said, "put ripples in the soup bowls of neighbours the length and breadth of Madison Avenue."

He next promised to line every inch of the house with felt. It might then be possible to have a conversation without the need to shout. Lastly, he unveiled a plan to dig a trench across the yard to divert steam from the generator to a special chimney in the garden. This would stop vapours from leaking through the floorboards, lending the plush living quarters the tropical atmosphere of the Everglades.

The Morgans agreed to every expense, but the irony was not lost on any at the table that this was a huge amount of upheaval and cost for the comparatively tiny advantage of having a diamond-friendly light available at the turn of a thumbscrew.

Mrs Morgan rose to retire. Morgan flicked her an irritated glance. Layered like an artichoke in taffeta, she floated away. When she was gone, Edison presented an even bolder suggestion. "Large public generators. That's what we actually need. Substations. Every few city blocks. Get the generators out of the houses. But it will cost."

"Just do it."

"You see, DC is very strong – but it falls away after a hundred yards. So we'll need a great number of substations per square mile—"

Morgan raised a hand. He didn't want the details. "Just get to work. We're not running out of money – not yet – but we are running out of time."

* * *

What a lesson Edison was to receive from Morgan in the tactics of aggressive commerce. Soon adopted as an intimate of the Astors, the Vanderbilts, the Havermeyers, and meeting Morgan each day in his boat or in some private club or at one of the gilt houses on Madison Avenue, he was gradually schooled in the strategies of the *new way of thinking*. Anxious, tireless in advancing his dream at any occasion, Morgan taught Edison to view life through a banker's eyes, envisaging a world run by a cadre of business elites, men of substance but of real principle too: the poor must not be forgotten in all this. Honourable professionals who must wrest power out of the hands of impotent and self-serving politicians only too willing to bend to the infuriating whims of their electorate. Edison listened, gave the appearance of agreeing with much of what Morgan said, nodding as few men have nodded, but within, down in some deep recess of character, he retained not only his cynicism, but his belief that there was a way to get what he wanted out of this relationship without being tainted for ever by it.

He had become a realist. And, as a realist, it was clear that it was possible to accept the advice and the earmarked dollars of the wealthy in order to do any good, while protecting that priceless part of you that was the source of all genuine creativity.

When free of Morgan's lectures Edison hurried downtown.

He felt the urge to roll up his sleeves. His men had begun building America's first public electrical substation on Pearl Street. No more domestic earthquakes, no more Everglades gases. Twelve huge generators would silently light the parlours and offices and diamond dinners of the Golden 100 set. But if the banker's money entered Edison's accounts like a stream, it also went out like a river, pushing the enterprise into credit relationships that soon strained the charter of many major lenders. Only Morgan's faith encouraged the banks to hold their nerve. Morgan was, simply, too respected to be wrong.

No rail trips back to New Jersey now. From Fifth Avenue the inventor rode only on the railcar downtown. Looking down from the elevated track, he surveyed the wooden slums, the swarming life of the immigrant streets choked with horse-drawn traffic, the sky dark with soot and more acrid substances – and the smell of coal and stench of rubbish piled beside the cast-cement stoops made him tug the window shut. All lay before him: the gas-lit streets awaiting modernity, the Western Union building where, as a younger man, he had perfected Wall Street's first stock-ticker machine; beyond it, visible, the Bowery, wilder blocks teeming, he knew, with seamen, bootleggers, card sharks, disgraced clergy with open collars, carpetbaggers, poor kids from Five Points and Mulberry Bend who, for a niggardly purse, would punch each other into a stupor in street-corner prize fights, transients of every stripe, émigrés all, human traffic cast adrift but washing up here in the upsurge of a fast-mutating metropolis. His streetcar stopped outside a Baptist Church converted, like so many others, into a gambling house – inside, a scene so habitual the details could be imagined: priestly vestments still hanging on the altar, the winning numbers being hailed by drunkards from the pulpit, fat New Jersey farmers with barking dogs in their laps spending their crop wealth on the spin of a wheel. And whilst shady business deals were finessed in the pews, whores provided emergency love in the choir loft.

THOMAS

"Feel it, son? Feel it?"

The old man then did something wholly mysterious in the boy's eyes: he planted the silver tip of his walking stick firmly into a crack in the station boards, closed his teeth on the top of the stock, then shut his eyes in concentration. "That's our train all right," he said, lifting the cane. "Are the tracks clear? My eyesight ain't so good any more. Tell me if the tracks are clear."

"Clear enough, sir."

"You sure?"

"Clear enough."

"Always make darn sure, son. I once saved a boy, a nipper three years old. Dashed into the path of an incoming train. Plucked him off the tracks m'self. Only your age, I was. I was the only one felt the train coming."

"Is that so?"

"That got me my first start. Ha!"

"You saved someone's life?"

The old man didn't reply. He withdrew into private thoughts, regressing sixty years to when he had been on a platform exactly like this one, seated with his ear to the crack of the telegrapher's shutters, deciphering an incoming telegraphic warning of a train's approach from the next station down the line. But he had been too absorbed in the code's formal beauty, too in thrall to its music to realize that a

ANTHONY McCARTEN

child, just then kicking stones on the tracks before him, was in great danger. Even as his eyes were on the toddler his thoughts were elsewhere. It was crazy to recall it now, but he had made no connection between the telegram and the child's urgent situation.

At this point in his life his adoration of Morse code had become a passion so great it eclipsed common reality, growing in inverse ratio to the deterioration of his hearing. Deaf to most low-level sounds since the age of seven, his interest in the code had become an obsession, and the seat outside the telegrapher's window was as hallowed to him as a pew in church was to his mother.

It was hardly his own fault. His father had earlier diagnosed water in the eardrum and forbidden Alva from taking a swim or a bath in six weeks. The only effect was to marginalize the youngster further, driving Alva to resort to the consolations of literature.

That was how, in the library of the Young Men's Society, he discovered Samuel F.B. Morse. He came across a biography and, alone in the library after hours, studied the codified system invented twenty-five years before. He fell for the stuttering beauty of the two-note alphabet. In his private world where no bird sang, where no cat protested for food, where trees were soundless and the riverboat paddles had no babble, and where the people on the main street of Port Huron were as silent to him as Trappist monks, he found with relief an exit from the chamber of his predicament and, as a second language can grow to supplant the original, becoming the vernacular of one's dreams, the high clear *click-click-click* of a telegraph key pierced his silent world. How grateful he was to find the one sound that reached him undiminished! It came in stops and starts: both sound and non-sound, noise and absence of noise...

Dot... dash... dot... dot... dot...

On that long-ago morning, with his ear to the telegrapher's window, Alva lost sight of the child as the train careered past. Had he seen

84

the boy carried off? The train seemed endless. He rose to his feet, the only witness to the event.

But the child was unharmed. When the train passed by, Alva was on the far side of the tracks in an instant, scooping the kid up in his arms, just at the moment when the child's father, J.U. McKenzie, the station master and telegrapher, came out onto the platform, shouting: "You saved his life!"

Did Alva take credit for doing so?

"It was nothing," Alva had replied. The station master embraced him, and later, in gratitude, offered Alva his first job.

"And that's how I got started in the telegraph business," the old man told the young one, sixty years after those events. "With that one little lie. And that job as a telegrapher led to everything else that came later."

As the young boy nodded, the old man sat gravely still for many long minutes, until he started to sniff the air loudly.

"You all right, sir?"

"Fish. I smell fish. You smell fish?"

EDISON

The odour of gutted fish, wafting in from the Fulton Market, made rank the air at the new substation where the building's interior was full of unbreathable coal dust. Edison workers had been slaving for weeks in temperatures of over 100 °F on six huge DC dynamos, building the world's first power station in downtown Manhattan. Stripping off his coat, shedding his new office persona, Edison joined these men, leapt into the heart of this industrial process, crawled on the floor, peered under the dynamos, made suggestions to the foremen while lying on his back among the filth. Rising, with a force field of some kind surrounding him so that his hair stood comically on end, he told his men there could be no talk of failure. His accounting work had made one thing clear: failure this time would put them all out of business.

But always the office called him back to daylight. Papers waited to be signed. Money men wished to see him. Back on Fifth Street, Morgan paid one of his surprise visits.

Astonished to see the chimney sweep before him, the banker cancelled the meeting and dragged Edison down to Park Avenue, where a London-trained tailor ran a tape up the inventor's instep and measured his brim size. Edison had retained the telegrapher's habit of gartering his sleeves: he was encouraged to abandon this. Surrendering at last his dusty Prince Albert coat and crumpled neckerchief, he tried on shirts and trousers. Onyx cufflinks were attached to his sleeves. Made over, he looked into the tailor's full-length mirror with the horror of a man who suddenly recognizes a loathsome quality in himself that he had not known, till now, existed.

Back on the street, in a shirt of starched wing collars, a bow tie, a shiny ascot, he made for the bar of the New York Yacht Club, where Morgan and Vanderbilt were waiting.

The banker jumped to his feet. "We're waiting for Mr Edison!" Vanderbilt barked. "Show this impostor out!"

Edison reddened, turned and left the room.

"Have I offended him?" Vanderbilt asked Morgan, who, equally mystified, shrugged.

But moments later, Edison was back. He had rumpled his hair and had taken a restaurant napkin and wrapped it around his neck. With a grin he shouted: "Pierpont, I've been looking for you everywhere!"

"Ah, Alva!" Morgan roared back through his own laughter. "The damnedest thing! We just had your counterfeit in here a minute ago, trying to pass himself off as the great inventor. I believe the fool was even wearing *cologne*. A travesty of verisimilitude."

Morgan had a rod-shaped gift for Edison, who tore off the wrapping to reveal a cane with a solid silver tip and a bone handle: the brother of Morgan's own. It carried on the stock the initials T.A.E. where on his own was written J.P.M.

Taking their cocktails, they settled into armchairs.

"So how was your first week, Alva?"

Edison sighed. "The office work of Fifth Avenue doesn't suit me, but the substation is going to work out, Pierpont. Also, my colleague, Charles Batchelor, is going to set up a factory from which municipalities will be able to order an entire network, from thirty-ton dynamos right down to chandeliers and individual bulbs."

"Wonderful, wonderful. Then everything is in place. Splendid, splendid. Now then, tell me, how are you finding the life of a businessman?"

"Repugnant. But necessary."

Morgan roared again. "My own feelings in a nutshell!" The banker ordered asparagus sandwiches. "Often more repugnant than necessary. I do enjoy your sense of humour, Alva. I've just been calling you the funniest man in New York."

"Funny by design or by accident?"

"Perhaps a combination of the two."

"Well, if it's a *combination*, then I'm not surprised J.P. Morgan enjoys it."

"There! Ha! Ha! You see? This quality of yours is quite unsung. Let's make it part of your image from now on."

"My image?"

"Now then, there's a couple of new matters that need your attention."

"Matters?"

"But first, I want you to explain to me the difference between… between 'direct current' and this… this new, what are they calling it?"

"The *difference*? Why do you ask?"

"Have you heard of… I think his name is… Nikola Tesla?"

"He used to work for me."

"Is he mad? Do you know?"

Edison shifted inside his new suit, feeling suddenly restricted under the arms, tight across the chest. "I suppose he might be. Why?"

"Then perhaps we have nothing to fear."

"Fear?"

"As a potential threat."

"Not at all. Why do you ask?"

"Because he's staging some sort of demonstration. Some grand demonstration of his alternative current."

"Alter-*nating* current."

"Yes, well let's hope it's not an alternative, shall we?"

* * *

"Ladies and Gentlemen. I now have the immense pleasure of introducing... a genius, who is shaking up the entire electrical field."

Thomas Alva Edison put his hands together and reluctantly joined in the applause that spread around the auditorium of the Institute of Electrical Engineers as the compère cried: "Nikola Tesla!"

Behind Edison, in the back row, skulked another national icon, the bullish George Westinghouse, a railway magnate. The man was not only applauding, but already shouting "Bravo!"

Through a side door marched the keynote speaker. What a figure Tesla really was! Six foot six, with a dandy's eye for a fine suit. He came to the stand, arranged his sheath of papers like a dean and began to list the shortcomings of direct current – the standard power that all of Edison's machines relied upon.

Edison listened with dismay and slowly increasing fury.

"Most distinguished colleagues. As you all know, electricity is generated by a rotating magnet inside a copper coil. A magnet it has two poles. One positif, the other negatif, and so the current that is generated it alternates also, positif and negatif, in cycles, or Herz, travelling along wires in waves. We know this as alternating current, or AC. But because no one ever know how to harness this current to run a motor, the current it has always been stored up, in the live wires themselves, in the dangerous form of direct current, or DC. An industry of inventions has springed up that can be run on nothing else. But Nikola Tesla is here to tell you... that DC is dead." To startled cries of "Dead?" and "Did he say dead?" he continued: "Yes. Direct current – *your* current – *all* of your current – is dead. A thing of the past. What is more, the public is being misled by certain of you – and the money men who are propping you up." Tesla moved an accusing finger across the front rows of the audience. "With your

DC system the long-distance transmission of power is a joke. Buried wires store the charge, and this charge it fall away after a few hundred feet, wasted or electrifying the very ground. Lunacy has a new face. And why, all of this? Because up until now no one is developing a motor that can run on AC. No one until Tesla. Tesla has now devised a revolution in the delivery of power."

Tesla paused for effect. Not embarrassed that he was using the techniques of the music hall rather than the science hall, Tesla then began to unveil his breakthrough with alternating current, previously thought too dangerous to handle. He went to the blackboard and parted a curtain. With a tap of his bony finger he indicated a diagram of circuits for an all-new system to replace the DC standard, one capable – he claimed – not only of safely delivering electrical current over hundreds of miles without any drop-off in power at all – a claim which drew gasps and some applause – but, at its end, of also driving – by this point an assistant had wheeled out a trolley holding something covered by a sheet, which Tesla pulled away – "an AC motor!" The audience once more broke into murmurs of awe and dissent. "The sun has long withheld its secrets," he finally declared, "but no longer!"

The audience became polarized at this point. Not everyone was persuaded. "You say a *motor*? Working on *alternating current*? But there can be no such invention."

"Not so." Tesla smiled triumphantly. "I haff just invented a motor myself. And it runs very well. But this will be the subject of my next lecture. Tesla is here today to demonstrate my new AC system, and to prove to you its safety beyond any doubt."

Edison could take no more and rose to his feet. Heads turned at once. "Mr Tesla – I advise you against such a demonstration. We are all here committed to direct current – but for scientific reasons, not monetary. I am here as a silent observer only, and have been largely unable to hear Mr Tesla's address due to a defect of the inner ear, but Mr Tesla well knows that I am an opponent of alternating current, and have been for a decade, ever since lengthy investigations showed me beyond a doubt that the problems in the alternating system are insoluble at best. Mr Tesla's claims, although entertaining, can be ignored."

Applause greeted this comment, but Tesla only smiled.

"Mr Thomas Edison! In this place of science you are wishing to prohibit debate? You of all people? An inventor? What is happening to your open mind?"

"You force me to go further, sir. Very well. Then let me say, and with as much certainty as I say that there is no danger at all to life, health or person in the current generated by an Edison dynamo, and various incidents have proved as much – why, even the poles of the direct-current generator can be grasped with the naked hand without the slightest effect! – then I am just as certain as death itself that the alternating system that this fella proposes tonight will git one customer a month killed if it's ever put in."

"Hear, hear," shouted a growing number of people in the crowd.

Tesla, however, was not to be cowed. "You cannot say your DC is safer! This cannot be said!"

"We all know more about direct current – that *makes* it safer. You can't take risks with people's lives. You can't just go storming out there with new untried technologies. Therein lies the danger." Edison's face had become red as he'd worked his way up to his final conclusion: "My personal desire would be to prohibit entirely the use of AC."

With this, Edison sat, and the clamour caused by his pronouncements took time to subside. So many issues suddenly concerned the crowd. Was Edison now a scientific conservative? Was he refusing to entertain new ideas in order to promote his own? If so, did this evening represent the death of open-minded enquiry in American science? Or was Tesla a madman? Were his ideas laughable, unworkable – indeed, even lethal?

Mr Tesla was given right of reply. The Serb, unshaken, bore a light smirk on his face. He said he did not mind losing his high opinion of Mr Edison as a scientist. "This great man has become an industrialist. Witness his closed mind, here, tonight." Over some booing, but quite a few chuckles, he then asked the clerk for the opportunity to demonstrate his claims. What better proof of AC's safety than a demonstration?

Before opinion could even be canvassed, the assistant helped Tesla out of his coat. He then rolled up his shirtsleeves so that wires could be wound around his elbows. Standing cruciform before his stunned audience, he looked less like a human guinea pig than a pseudo-messiah. The wires fed back to what Tesla explained was a hand-cranked AC generator and an air-core transformer of his own design, able to reduce dangerous amperage to levels of safety never before dreamt of. As he spoke, the assistant set up a voltmeter in front of him. He then asked for the gaslights to be trimmed, and was granted this last courtesy without demur, for there was a risk in most minds that this man might kill himself tonight.

"I will now proof beyond a shadow of a doubt the better safety of my system. And I will show the overnight conservatives that direct current must be consigned to history!"

Tesla was ready. The assistant cranked the dynamo, slowly at first but with increasing speed, as Tesla, watching the meter, told the audience that he would inform them at intervals of how much voltage was passing through his body. With this rule established, and with current already travelling through him, he chided them further. The lifeblood of science was heresy! Only thugs and businessmen could afford to annihilate competition. Real progress was born out of the war of ideas and their antithesis, opinion shifting back and forth, changing direction as needs be, oscillating, alternating, like the fires on the sun! Only from this was real progress born!

With no change to his demeanour, he announced that the 10,000-volt mark had just been passed.

The alternating current surged into him.

Then the 20,000 mark… and the 50,000… the 100,000, and then – fighting to remain calm, his limbs beginning to shudder, the sinews on his neck to stand out – the 150,000 mark! He was a madman. In his determination to legitimize his radical ideas, trying to show no ill effects, it was increasingly clear to the audience that with 10,000 times the voltage a person could be expected to withstand coursing through him, the scientist was approaching – no, exceeding – the limits of endurance. His body vibrated. His shoes shook. His hands were clenched into fists. His jaw chattered, and when he spoke next it was with gritted teeth. "Two… hundred… thousand," Tesla exclaimed, his long face now crimson under the strain.

"Enough, sir. Desist! That is quite enough!" The president of the Institute jumped to his feet.

"This is madness!" the Mayor of New York barked.

But Tesla had a number in his head now, and his sights were set on reaching it. With cables of high tension braiding his neck, he turned awkwardly to his assistant and incited him with a nod to crank even faster. Scientific fists struck tables. Charged electrons coursed through Tesla's blood, and he turned back to the audience only when he felt he had reached the threshold of life itself.

"Two… hundred… and fifty… thousand!" He could hardly get the last word out.

Some suspected chicanery and rushed forward. Such a voltage was impossible to withstand. They inspected the dial, but turned back to nod to the cynics. The dial supported Tesla's claim. "It's true."

building, filling a copper cable (hemp-bound, rubber-coated, laid a dead man's depth underground along a scar of new cobbles across the city), electrons racing through it, the charge breaking out of the great dynamo room at a speed of starlight, flowing under the soles of Erastus Woodbury, the City Commissioner of Public Works, standing anxious at the gate, overseeing these first nervous moments, then streaming directly up the street under the horse carts, drays, landaus and broughams, coursing via the interred threads and at 1,000 miles a second under the haunches of the fishmonger Gorman O'Grady, before turning left by the elm dying of Dutch blight on Grayson Street, bisecting, unseen, underneath the leather boots of the Bohemian flower-seller with her wilting buckets of peonies unsold at this evening hour, launching left then, at an angle of forty-five degrees, past O'Corkles Bar and on the hypotenuse shooting up Bristol Street like many a drinker before it, making directly for the central business district, where, at the Provost Avenue Junction Box, the main line frayed, multiplied, fanned out, forty wires thereafter making for other junction boxes, fostering more offshoots until four hundred wires more or less swerved and wound their way indoors and by serpentine wrigglings insinuated themselves into the walls and ceilings and the very fixtures of the genteel lamps of the city's first lighting district. Light! A miracle! Every bulb went wonderfully aglow. In a second the night-time city was lit by the work of dynamic faradization, bulbs burning safely in every fixture on Elkington Avenue, safely burning in the high houses and in the counting houses of Reece Street, shining bright even in Madame de Ausprey's boudoir on Farrah Square and in the street lamps above the children playing ring-a-ring-o' roses round every pole on Fenimore Street, a gentle, warm, darkness-dispelling glow, and all fears fading at light speed as a cheer goes up: a success, a triumph, a city ablaze! Where was the inventor? Aldermen found him, surrounded him, placed their own orders. For Chicago, Buffalo,

Boston, Poughkeepsie. All would be lit by the inventor. *Hip-hip* – hats flew – *hurray!* His name became a chant. It echoed, drifting upward above the day-bright buildings into the black night…

"Westinghouse!… Westinghouse!… Westinghouse!"

* * *

At his now customary table in a cordoned-off area of Delmonico's Restaurant, Edison lowered the *New York Post* with the bitter resignation of a man who has woken to find himself in possession of a life that was no longer his own. Westinghouse! This thief had robbed him of his own triumphant moment and lit Greensburg, Pennsylvania, before he could light Manhattan. Westinghouse! As a swan-tailed waiter set before him a plate of *huîtres à la provençale*, he wondered what damage Tesla's victory – establishing AC as the first current to light up an American city – would do to his own plans.

The only outright sign of distress in his face was the inflammation of his eyes. He lit one of Morgan's own brand of cigar, a new habit: two more of these cigars were poked in his top pocket over his own monogrammed handkerchiefs. He drew deeply and sent out a plume into the room which, when it cleared, revealed to him… a gaslight fitting, still burning on the wall of this New York club.

He rose. He had a meeting, an urgent one. Morgan was waiting at the New York docks. He made his way out into the thronging streets, raised his cane to separate the crowds when they threatened to push in on him too tightly. He was late and walked quickly under the webs of telegraph wires and between the horse-drawn traffic.

In the shadow of a giant ocean liner, dressed in the white suit of a tycoon on the Grand Tour, J.P. Morgan was prowling among a hundred artefacts unpacked from wooden crates: white statuettes, pots, plaster fountains, alabaster sphinxes, Coptic lions in stone, temple relief blocks, ceramic urns, sarcophagi, Egyptian clay cats, granite busts of Rameses II and miniature pharaonic needles. He was furious. His buying trip for antiquities had been a disaster.

"How did you know I was back?" he barked as Edison approached.

"You sent a message. I came right away. How are you?"

"Awful. None of this is what I paid for. None of it. The Egyptians have hoodwinked me. They packaged up second-rate fakes. They think I can't tell the difference, you see. Because I'm American, of course. They wouldn't try this with an Englishman, but they think an American will buy anything."

"Is that what they think?"

"And they're right, of course. It's quite true. We *will* buy anything. Carnegie and Vanderbilt are sitting on mountains of garbage. It's part of being a new country, you see. It takes decades to develop any culture at all, but it takes centuries to develop any taste. But they underestimate *me*. They forget my credentials. I am not your average American."

Indeed he was not. Morgan walked away and began a conversation with a shipping agent who was coming down the gangway of the *Germanic*, no doubt expecting a storm. Morgan's walking stick, held as a club, looked poised to strike at any minute, and only the agent's grovelling prevented an assault. Edison moved closer to overhear the reason of the dispute. With his poor hearing he had to come very close indeed.

"I don't care if they're *authentic*, you fool! The point is they don't *look* authentic! That is the difference! *That* is the difference. And no, sir, you shall not pack them up and ship them back. Why should I bear the added expense of that? My chances of a refund are zero as it is. So what am I to do? If this junk cannot go back and cannot stay, then I have a much better idea."

Morgan's eyes sparkled. He walked into the centre of the consignment and with the butt of his cane began to thrash his way through the relics, staving in ancient heads, turning Gods into amputees, reducing the most fragile pieces to fragments. The agent dared not look as the banker went about the task, and in minutes the American had reduced a million dollars' worth of relics to a white pile of dust.

Crimson-faced, his terrible nose a purple beacon – motes of white plaster clinging to its sebaceous surface – Morgan walked back up to the poor wretch and uttered two words:

"Business concluded."

The cane came down on the dock, and the banker walked off in the direction of Wall Street. Edison hurried to catch up. As they entered the black tide of businessmen, Morgan appeared to Edison a great white shark from whose path the minnows scattered.

* * *

Inside the Drexel-Morgan building, in Morgan's transparent glass office, the inventor was told:

"We have to ruin Westinghouse."

Edison stared at the banker, uncomprehending. "How do you mean *ruin*, exactly?"

"Ruin. Crush him. Before it's too late. Find a way."

"I don't understand."

"Discredit him, both him and his alternating current. And do it quickly." Morgan brushed white dust off his sleeve. "Turn him into this stuff. I leave it up to you."

"But this… err… this is hardly my field."

"Make it your field. Use that imagination of yours. Invent a way, sir. Or else we're done here. Done." He clapped his hands together. More dust rose.

Edison considered his response. "My skill is to make something work that doesn't work. Yours is to wreck something that does. Forgive me, but... how can I discredit this current when, at least for now, it's proving so successful?"

Morgan gave him a sharp look. "His current is *not* successful. Don't ever think it. It's a failure that we simply need to prove."

"But their system is fifty per cent cheaper than ours. And a hundred and thirty towns and cities are already in talks to adopt it."

Morgan shook his head, losing patience with his protégé. "Stop! Stop right there! There you go again. Seeing things from the other side. Shape up, Tom. There's too much money on the table now to think like this. I expect you to dominate this market. Establish DC as the market standard."

"Of course."

"*Dominate* it, sir! Dominate it." Morgan even slammed his fist down on the table. "We can't horse around for another moment, not a single second. And you must turn on the lights in Manhattan at once."

"We need more testing."

"At once."

* * *

Act? Dominate? Destroy? How? How did one go about this?

On Madison Avenue, Edison and his assistant Charles Batchelor were conferring as they walked.

"But how am I supposed to do it?"

Batchelor had no answer.

Edison took out a cigar and lit it.

At the Pearl Street substation, still some weeks from being ready, the one-time inventor announced that they would turn the power on and light the Central Business District in three days.

His men nodded. None protested, not one spoke against the idea.

Later, alone, Edison sat sweltering in the heat watching a worker shovel slag into a raging furnace, one spadeful after another, the man's naked torso shiny with his own grease, the fire leaping with each new addition. *How am I meant to know how to destroy another's man's invention?* How was such destruction enacted? To ruin the work of another colleague was against the rules of scientific practice. One could disprove someone else's theory, or render a rival's invention obsolete by surpassing it with something better, but in the absence of this, how did one *ruin* a competitor? And what would his hero, Michael Faraday, think of this? Or his beloved Tom Paine, whose religion was ever "to do good"? Somehow he must find fault with AC – somehow see a weakness in it, a flaw. And while doing this unpalatable work, he must also keep his eye on his high, original purpose. What had he told his workers once? *Any successful invention was a divine extrapolation of nature* – yes, that was it. And he still believed this. *A snowflake under a microscope, a fob watch, a water pump – all draw from the same universal blueprint.* He had quoted Leibniz and the Theosophists to these working men and women, calling the work on the electric lamp *religious*, reminding them in a fit of rhetoric that *the Sumerians saw light as the outer garment of God.* Yes, he must remain true to all of this, even while discrediting the Westinghouse-Tesla system. His ethics were deeply ingrained. He was confident, strong, celebrated. He'd been called upon to be an example to others. His conscience was clear. He felt certain he could balance these two missions.

* * *

At last, Edison and Morgan stood under the street lamp. One reporter and one photographer had come to witness the moment. The mood was maudlin.

"Not quite the exhibition I had anticipated," Morgan grumbled.

"Lighting the entire central business district of lower Manhattan for the first time with the pull of one lever is no small feat."

"We should have been the first, the first to light a US city. Nobody is interested in second place. Second place is the first loser." He stared at the street lamp more intensely and adjusted his glasses. "And why are we doing this at noon? Might not the effect have been enhanced with a little darkness?"

"I have never pretended to be P.T. Barnum."

Morgan snorted. "P.T. Barnum you are not, sir! One reporter. Ha! You may not require publicity, but I can assure you my investors do. And they are about to mutiny. Mutiny. We are losing the fight."

Edison consulted his fob watch. "Here we go. I shall count down. Ten, nine, eight…"

"This had better work."

"Five, four, three, two, one – *there*!"

Both men and the reporter stared at the street lamp as the photographer took his picture. Edison turned to look both ways up Wall Street.

"Is it working?" Morgan asked.

"It's going… I believe."

"Is that it? Oh for Heaven's sake!"

Edison climbed the stepladder to inspect the bulb as Morgan called up, "I rather hope it isn't going." The change in the lamp was imperceptible.

The reporter stepped forward. "Sir? May I have a comment?"

"Yes," Morgan rasped, spinning around and smiling, raising his nose as the photographer prepared a second photograph. "I am overwhelmed. Foul odious gaslight has been vanquished for ever. Long live the future. A bright future, under Edison Electric Light. That's… Edison Electric Light."

Edison had good news from the top rung. "Yes. It burns. It's working."

"There you are. Success! Success." But under Morgan's great moustache the thick lips then moved again, and these words were for himself. "I can hardly contain myself."

* * *

Edison took a late train back to New Jersey, jumping on a coal tender at 4 a.m. and riding, as he used to as a youngster, with the engineer.

He breathed deeply the cold night air, hoping it would revive him, and his boyhood days returned: of selling newspapers on the Port Huron-Detroit line at eight years old; going home to his parents' vegetable farm, where his mother home-educated him. His interests were so scientific even then that his worried father paid him a penny for every novel he read. With this money, however, he bought yet more scientific books.

As the engineer shovelled coke into the furnace, Edison watched the leafless trees, dark cracks on the starlit sky, and recalled the first telegraph system he ever built, a line of stovepipe wire strung up between his parents' backyard and his friend's yard next door. Two apple trees served as telegraph poles. Down this line he and his best friend, Jim Clancy, practised their Morse, sending and receiving the day's news, or speeches from Shakespeare. In his early teens by then, Al would forsake the baseball games and the walks home with girls to sit at the stationmaster's shoulder, watching as the news reports of the Civil War came in. In those days Al was far from being able to take down the news, which was dispatched by the best senders and came in too fast, but it was this to which he aspired. On the rare occasion when he was permitted to stay in the depot after hours, and when a war dispatch came in, he picked up a pen and, from the torrential clatter of Morse, reduced to five days the Seven Days' Battle of Richmond, or gleaned that there had been a second battle at Bull Run but not the outcome. With the skeins of the telegraph wire now his central nervous system, he felt compelled to join the Confederates and give his life as other young men his age would soon do at Gettysburg, Cold Harbor and Petersburg.

But then his father would come in, with a coat over his pyjamas, to take him home, telling him war was the bastard child of politics, a contrivance reliant for its existence on the passions of the easily stirred. "The time for armies is ending." Alva should concentrate on being a genius instead.

How Edison missed his father now. A true eccentric, Sam had built the family house with his own hands, then added a tower for good measure. Whenever Alva walked home from the station he could see the old man up there, a hundred feet above the house, scouring the landscape for omens of war. But with the sound of musketry many thousands of miles away and moving farther off every day, he was a forlorn sight. He had built the tower on a mad whim, wanting to sell to tourists to Port Huron, at twenty-five cents a pop, tickets for a panoramic view of the listless lumber town below, and thus provide the Edison family with a modest income. But the demand for any kind of view of the log-choked, insect-infested Black River was non-existent. And so this anti-war man, slowly losing his marbles, and still dropping hints that he was "under orders", working for dissident factions, fulfilled his phantom investiture by remaining aloft many hours each day, at the service of "the people", awaiting the hostilities that alone could now justify the entire folly. Avoiding him in those days – children yearn for fathers to be normal – Alva fled his chores and, in his backyard cave, sent and received passages from *Macbeth* with Jim

Clancy. Knees drawn up to his chin in the hand-dug hollow, he lowered copper electrodes into jars of acid: a crude battery. The telegraph was ready; the line alive. With an amateur hand Alva warned Jim to beware the time when *Great Birnam wood* should come to *Dunsinane*.

Which got him his first paid job for Western Union.

By this time, Al had already decided to place himself in the service of the people – "his religion to do good" – and to plead the human argument: people first. All great individuals must first be poets, Tom Paine wrote: henceforth exult the imagination! Intoxicated with virtue, Alva read *The Age of Reason* by candlelight in his little bed under the stairs.

"What's going on?" his mother asked him one night, stopping by his bedroom, her lips turned down at the edges, a tic she had passed on to her son. Since the death of a third child in two years she now dressed permanently in black. "What is all this?"

Alva's room was now stuffed with boxes of feathers, rubber, cornstalk pitch, bottled acids, mercury, beeswax, alum, rags, tin, corks, sulphur, lead, nails, wire, to name but a few of the products he was hoarding. The young man hoped by their mere accumulation he would intuit the recipe by which he might magically combine them to create something useful to the human race. But so far, nothing. The room was a stinking mess.

"Get this foul stuff to the basement now," his mother shouted.

Alva moved to the basement, and to the orange flicker of an oil lamp willed genius upon himself. Underground, he worked as though a recording angel were at his shoulder, weighing his every deed against the greatest works of men as he combined a tincture of one powder and a pinch of another.

The explosion blew off the storm shutters. A shoehorn with Sam's insignia was found a quarter-mile away.

In the last fizzing moment before the flash, Al had dived for cover.

"Oh Rinkey," Al's adoring sister, Harriet, lamented as she had tended the blackened boy. "Why did you have to go and do that? You know Mama can't stand to lose another one of us. We both just have to stay alive. No more dying, please. We have to live for ever. Promise me that."

Harriet died that year, haemorrhaging in childbirth. At the end of her funeral, saying little and hearing nothing from the front pew, he set a single white carnation on her casket. Under his arm a book people presumed to be the Bible. It was, in fact, Faraday's *Experimental Researches in Electricity and Magnetism*.

On the steaming train the now famous inventor remembered again his long-ago promise to his sister. But it was she who, in her request, had miscalculated. Life, he wanted to tell her now, was merely a minor electromagnetic event. The human force, magnetized into human shape, did not bear our names for long. Draped in clothes and circumstance and culture, the individual might teeter, dance, plead its case for a brief moment, but sooner or later the Universe exerted its invincible force and pulled apart this "freak event" (in Faraday's words). This was the trivial circuit of life and death. Outside this circuit? Our eternal home.

But of course, Harriet had long known all this at first hand.

These thoughts were occupying the inventor as the train skidded into Menlo Park.

Climbing the hill to his house he had forgotten his house keys, so opted to swing his legs up onto the upper veranda and enter his bedroom by the first-floor window.

His wife, waking, pulled a loaded handgun out from under her pillow, called out "Who is it?" three times as the sash window rose, and then fired. As the bullet took out a huge chunk of the window frame, she saw a body drop out of sight onto the roof with a heavy thud.

Her thumb pulled back the hammer of the Peacemaker: she was ready to fire again. "Show your face!..."

But when she turned on her new bedside electric lamp, she heard only a muffled voice from the roof.

"Mary."

"Who is it?"

"What in God's name are you doing?!"

"Go away or I'll shoot."

With this, a hand came into view and waved. "Mary, it's me. It's me!" Finally Edison rose and stepped in the window. "Put the goddamn gun down. What do you think you're playing at?"

But Mary wouldn't lower the Peacemaker even then. "How do I know it's you? My husband lives in New York."

"You've been taking too much bromide."

"I've forgotten what he looks like. How do I know you're him? Tell me something only he would know."

"What sort of game is this? What's up with you?"

"Prove to me at once that you're him, or I'll shoot."

With her loaded revolver aimed at his chest, he had little choice. And he deserved this treatment anyway. He hadn't contacted her in nineteen days, so taken up had he been with the electrification of New York. So on the foot of the bed he tapped a message in Morse.

Watching his finger, and hearing his wedding band resonate on the oak, she deciphered the incoming wire, understanding it word by word. Finally she lowered the weapon. He had just resent her the telegram of his marriage proposal, tapped onto her telegraph key by him when she'd been a novice telegraph operator.

"Do you remember?" he asked.

Her eyes became moist. "And have you?"

"What?"

"Been 'thinking of me considerably of late'?"

"Of course. Of course."

"No you haven't."

She began to sing wistfully:

> "I am a 'elpless female,
> An unprotected female,
> My husband's been and gone...
> I'm left alone to sing.
> Oh, my Popsy Wopsy's vanished from my sight,
> And we might have been so happy – so we might."

Tears came to her eyes, and she didn't wipe them away. "I'm sorry."

"No, I'm sorry. I've been caught up. The lighting of New York... there's been difficulties. And you know very well I have to push the lamp, or else be robbed once again by the pirates." He shrugged, a fatigued man just shot at. "But if I can handle this right, I'll force everyone else out of the market. I've got a chance to dominate the whole field."

"Dominate? Is this the new talk in New York now?"

Edison sat beside her, took her hand tenderly, remembered that the "new talk" was out of place here. "I know what I'm doing. I'm only going to go so far. But it's this... Tesla, this young man Tesla. Used to work for me. Now he's bounding onto every music-hall stage in the land putting massive voltages through himself, trying to show that AC poses no danger, while proclaiming DC a killer. But it's trickery. Any scientist'll tell ya. All he did was change the amperage. You can have as many hertz and volts as you want. If the amperage is low, it won't kill ya. You understand, don't you?"

She nodded. "It *hertz* to amplify the volts."

He smiled gently, with love. "Indeed it does." On the verge of speech, he decided to tap a message on the floorboards with his right shoe.

She listened, then shook her head. "No you don't. If you loved me you'd be at my side."

"Popsy. This work is—"

"I know it's important."

"If it's not done right—"

"I know. What are the needs of one bedroom beside the whole world?"

"Please, don't say such things. They haunt me, Mary."

"Something strange – is affecting me. Some... force. I can't even read a poem any more. The doctors think I may be going mad."

"I see no evidence of that."

He smiled. But she couldn't smile back. Deep undiagnosed troubles were altering her. She felt their terrifying approach. At twenty-eight she was already feeling frail. "Don't joke. I am. I'm going mad."

Just then the bulb filament gave out and put them both in darkness.

"Then that makes two of us," Edison finally replied.

* * *

Two days later Mary was dead.

* * *

He was the last person to arrive at her bedside before the undertakers took her body away.

"I'm sorry, Al," the doctor whispered into his ear as he swept past. "There was nothing we could do."

Tears began to stream from Edison's eyes. "Let me talk to her! Let me talk to her!"

The doctor raised his voice. "Al, she's gone. She's gone."

"What are you talking about?"

"Congestion of the brain. I'm so sorry. She's gone." The look on the doctor's face conveyed what his words had not.

Alva stared back at him. "Gone?" But how could she have declined so fast? Why hadn't he been alerted? Word should have been sent to New York. His thoughts raced, keeping grief at bay. "What do you mean 'gone'? Why wasn't I told? What kind of doctor are you? Git out of here! From now on I'm... I'm going to look after her myself!"

The doctor remained where he was, knowing the vital importance of ignoring the outbursts of the suddenly bereaved.

Dropping to his knees at her bedside, the inventor took up his wife's hand. Mary had taken on the colour of death already, but Alva couldn't accept that he was too late to speak his mind, and so, as he had done a thousand times, he cradled her hand in his own. "Mary, can you receive?" On the back of her hand he tapped a coded message, dispatching on the cold skin a belated telegram.

It was only Mary's failure to reply that brought home her departure and made him face at last his loss. His eyes filled again. "Mary? You were the best part of me. What will I do now? Who can I talk to? Who will send me messages now?"

The doctor stepped close, laid a hand on his shoulder. "Let her go now, Al."

"She's trying to tell me something."

"Let her go."

But Al's hand still trembled over his wife's. "Speak to me. Send again." He said to the doctor: "She's trying to reach me! Her spirit is still here, it's strong. Mary? Send again. Send again, Popsy. What is it, Mary? I can't hear you. She's... trying to tell me something."

For half an hour he remained there, on his knees at the bedside. The doctor retired, but eventually returned.

Edison's face was now wet with tears as he said, "If I could... it's just a question of... of sensitivity. If I had a... something to capture... something to... Her spirit is still here."

"Really?"

"It's quite strong still. I'm sure if I measured her body's electrical resistance it would be unchanged from yesterday. Isn't that proof of something?"

The doctor, unfamiliar with electricity, nodded. "She is at peace now. Leave her be now, Mr Edison."

"She is still angry with me. I can feel it."

The doctor kept his level look. "Why do you think so? I saw her at the last. Believe me, she has found some peace of her own again."

It was a pointed remark. *Peace of her own?* But both men knew it was deserved. The inventor had denied this woman's heart any peace from the moment he had sent it tip-tip-tapping with a message in a telegraph office thirteen years before. And he had done his best over the years to wear it out ahead of time by leaving her to send her own signals of marital distress, each as unheeded and futile as those he had sent to her now at her deathbed.

It was Edison's turn to suffer, and he accepted it. He willed it upon himself. "Yes. You're right. I'll let her be. Poor darling."

He kissed her eyes and whispered, "Goodbye Popsy." Only when the doctor left for good did he notice her most recent bedside book, the poems by Christina Rossetti, lying open. He picked it up and read where his eye fell:

> *Too late for love, too late for joy.*
> *Too late, too late!*
> *You loiter'd on the road too long.*
> *You trifled at the gate:*
> *The enchanted dove upon her branch,*

Died without a mate;
The enchanted princess in her tower
Slept, died, behind the grate;
Her heart was starving all this while...
You made her wait.

Something broke inside him. He closed the book and tapped one last message on her hand, two words: "Forgive me".

"Mary?" he said, then waited. "Mary?"

"Mr Edison?" Mary's Spanish maid was standing behind him.

"What is it?"

"Come now. The children, they need you."

"Her spirit is still here, Margarita." He turned back to Mary. "It's strong."

"Yes. I feel it too." The maid made the sign of the Cross.

The two older children sat in the nursery, where the new baby slept. Pale, silent, their grief was inexpressible. Opening his arms, Dot and Dash ran into his embrace, as the baby with closed eyes gurgled unintelligible things in its blue crib.

Around midnight he went to his study and locked the door. He sat in utter silence until the Dresden wall clock chimed 2 a.m., then took out a notebook. While his wife lay two rooms away in the death pose, he started to draw lines, spirals, circuits, symbols. Desperate things flew onto the paper, his mind making unexpected leaps as he tried to design an invention to allow the living to communicate with the dead. That was what he would do now. Find a way to speak with Mary once more. With Mary, and thus with all the dead.

THOMAS

The inventor had the hue of a man who would never be well again. He had lost a lot of weight since his eightieth birthday. His skin fell in scrolls from his face and ruffled in an accordion under his chin. His eyes were milky. Breathing itself was a labour hardly worth the effort. To survive the next few minutes, he reached into his pocket and took out the plug of chewing tobacco, one his wife had failed to confiscate. He broke off a corner.

The young man joined the old one on the bench again. The old man looked once more up the tracks and squinted his worn-out eyes, saying, "Gonna be a big fuss right here on this platform in a minute."

"A big fuss, sir?"

"Don't you read the papers?"

"No, sir."

"Good for you. Ain't nothing in them you can trust anyway."

"That so?"

"I oughta know."

The youth's eyes sparkled. "You've been in the papers?"

The old man seemed content to just chew his foul-smelling plug, before replying, "In the papers you say? I been in them."

"Really? Are you famous then?" The boy looked into the old man's face, recognizing him as being at least ten very famous people, but not being quite able to decide yet which one.

The old man thought for a second more as to how to reply to this. "Once or twice." He left it at that. "And believe me, that's once or twice too often. Some advice: if the reporters don't make it up, then the folks that they're reporting on do. Between reporters and the kind of people that get reported on, truth doesn't git a chance."

The boy nodded. He was beginning to enjoy these cautionary pieces of wisdom, and whether the old man was famous or just deranged, it was surely a youth's duty to listen to the last lines of the soon-to-be-gone. "I wanna be in the papers some day."

"Then you will be."

The kid's eyes sparkled. "So what've *you* been in it for?"

"Forget about that."

The boy obliged with a long silence, until the old man volunteered: "For just about everything, if you wanna know."

"Really? Like what?"

The old man looked once more into the distance for the train that would bring all the world's press. "Killing people, for one thing. Been in the papers a few times for that."

The boy's eyes widened. "Killing people?"

"You bet. First time I was in a paper I was barely five years old."

"Five years old when you killed someone?"

The boy would have waited many hours to hear what the old man was to say next, but he only had to wait about a half-minute and tolerate three expulsions of tobacco spit onto the platform. "Went exploring this canal. Me and Toby Lockwood, a year younger'n me. Anyway, I had this idea of going swimming, 'cept I could hardly swim. And Toby took the idea right off me, but he couldn't swim at all. So I git scared and climb out all right, but Toby don't. Toby can't. And there it is. I watch the whole thing go on. And then – I just walked home, trailing a stick, and I go upstairs and git right under the covers. I'm cold and wet, shaking all over, and Mother comes in and tells me the Lockwoods are downstairs for me. Toby hadn't come home. His folks was clear out of their wits. They want to know if I know where Toby is, as I was the last one who'd seen him. By then the whole of Milan was out with their lanterns swinging looking all over for him. So I told 'em they could stop looking, cos Toby was gone, and I knew where he was all right. I told 'em what'd happened and what I'd done. Done, and not done."

The old man turned his eyes to the young man. An unresolved anger came over his features. "I had to watch him go down – Toby – I stayed for that. And I didn't go for help. Didn't speak. Nothing. Didn't even feel much, either. Was only five myself as I stood there and watched. Maybe I didn't even think it was a bad thing. I didn't think it was anything. But after something like that, it never stops coming back. All it does. Comes back. Old age is where everything that went out of you comes looking for you again."

"He drowned?"

"I already told you he did. What's the matter with you? Are you stupid? I saw it all, saw his head go down, watched him fight, saw his head go under and come up again and under, thrashing with his arms – I'm telling you what I see every day now – Toby trying to climb the water like it was a ladder, a ladder with no rungs. I saw him struggle for not too long and then he slipped under and then silence."

The boy hesitated a long while before speaking again. "So that was the first time…"

"What's that?"

"There were other… there were other times?"

"Other times?"

Reluctantly Edison thought again of his nephew Charley, his older brother's boy, placed in Edison's care when the kid was nine, but who died at nineteen. A first-rate inventor in his own right, perhaps even Edison's successor, Charley had died in Paris having been sent to

London by Edison to present his new telephone to the Royal Society. A boy of barely nineteen. Edison held himself responsible, and in complex ways, for Charley had died painfully, and of unexplained torments, at precisely the same time as he and his Menlo Park team had their great breakthrough with the lamp. Always looking for higher meanings, and willing to see a universal principle at work here, the boy's death and the birth of the lamp could be no coincidence. Prior to the creation of anything new – and in tune with Faraday's law on the preservation of energy – something had to be sacrificed, transmuted, whether heat, mass or motion.

"There were others?" the long-necked boy asked again, more loudly.

"Others?" The old man lifted his head as if regaining consciousness. "Ah, forget what I said. Maybe you should work for a newspaper. You got the right kind of stupidity. I said I've killed a lot of people, but I've told you all I'm going to tell you. Goddamn it, I'm trying to save some energy here."

The boy was shaken from the sudden volume, and wasted no time escaping to the other end of the platform.

EDISON

The corpse lay on the living-room floor. Neighbours knelt around it. The man, an employee of Edison General Electric, had been laying cables in trenches near Broadway. There had been an accident. The lines had been live. Death had been instantaneous.

In this worker's house, Edison found himself going down onto his knees. The eyes of Mr Jack Clarke were closed, and he looked peaceful enough, though the jaw was askew, as if badly set after a break, and his skin had a purplish hue, as though death had been brought on by the cold. His right palm was black.

Lately Edison had lost touch with the majority of his workforce, and Jack Clarke was therefore a stranger, merely one of the hundreds working under the Edison banner. He felt emotion well up within him, but he suppressed it. It would not be appreciated here.

He said a few short prayers, then rose. On the way out, Mrs Clarke stopped him and surprised him, thanking him for coming.

"He died for a good cause, if that's any comfort," Edison said. "He was bringing people progress."

The woman looked him straight in the eye. "Progress? Tell that to my children."

Edison returned to his office.

At his desk, loaded with unread paperwork, he was disturbed by the arrival of Morgan.

"Thomas? Listen. You need to get back to work. Do you hear me? That's what you need now."

"I abandoned her. I broke her heart. I'm responsible."

"Work is the best cure. Times like this. She gave you three children. Time to repay such a blessing. Yes?"

"'For what is a man profited if he shall gain the whole world and lose his own soul? Or what shall a man give in exchange for his soul?'"

"Steady now. Steady as she goes. You have nothing to blame yourself for. Take comfort, as I do, in remembering that certain people are called to carry a cross, to suffer for the sake of the many. Some, such as we, are denied the common comforts. Let me guide you."

"I have no one to talk to now. The line is cut! I AM A DEAF MAN! I AM CUT OFF NOW!"

Morgan gripped Edison firmly by the shoulders. "Stop it! Stop it now!"

"She was my connection…"

"You have *work* to do. Good work. Hear me? Great work. Noble work. CAN YOU HEAR ME, MAN?" Morgan's huge voice penetrated, finally, Edison's torture, and the inventor nodded, docile, compliant, desperate.

"What shall I do? Tell me. What shall I do? Eighty decibels. Tell me loudly."

"Stay the course. You hear? Come and see me. I'll send a coach. I must go. Yes?"

"Yes."

"Capital. I'm your friend. Now work. Remember? Work!"

"You're right."

When Morgan was gone, Edison returned to his desk. "Work. You're right."

But he had barely begun to focus his mind on this task when he was interrupted again, this time by the presentation of a letter of introduction.

The gilt letterhead announced the New York State Legislature.

"How can I help? I'm afraid I only have five minutes."

"Harold J. Brown, at your service."

Brown was a vaguely supercilious creature in a serge suit – his hair flattened with shellac – an engineer who had woken from a ten-year slumber to devote himself with frightening zealotry to proving the dangers of a modern enemy: electricity. Now he sought the great man's endorsement.

Edison erupted: "Are you a fool? Do I look like an opponent of electricity?"

The man smiled weakly and asked to be allowed to make himself more clear. "I understand your reputation, of course. Who doesn't? But you are also on record as saying you have had a lifelong dread of accidental death by electricity. Is it true you have never had an electrical shock yourself?"

Edison shrugged.

Brown looked triumphant. "Well *I* have. That began my crusade. And my findings show that at present we lack a safe form for electrical delivery."

Edison controlled his anger. "Your findings?" The "shock" this man had received must have rattled his wits. He was clearly a fool, a charlatan posing as an expert for the purposes of employment. "Brown. Let's not waste each other's time. My every effort right now is to prove the *safety* of electricity. Do you understand? We are adversaries. Now, I'm very busy."

"Sir," Brown continued. "I have with me six affidavits from eye-witnesses to electric shocks suffered by the public. One concerns a hearse which passed over a newly covered trench laid last week by the Maxim company of New York, which I understand has just been given the contract to light Broadway."

"This never happens with Edison lines."

"Still, while testing their lines a horse drawing a hearse reared up on its hind legs and—"

"Thank you. Good day." Edison returned to study his papers, but Brown did not take the hint.

"It is my aim, sir – indeed my mission, Mr Edison – to show the public the dangers at present inherent in electricity, and at the same time to find a way to use it for the public good. I am not a regressionist."

Edison stopped, looked up and laughed at this naked contradiction. "You make no sense, man. If it is dangerous, as you say, then how should it be used for the public good?"

"For criminal justice. Yes. I believe it would have a wonderful use."

"What use?"

"To electricide criminals, sir. That is a perfectly good use for it."

Edison put down the letter in his hand and abruptly showed the man to the door. "That is a repulsive idea. And you are a buffoon. Please leave me in peace. Sometimes I wish I was more deaf than I am."

"Well, while you have ears you must hear me out, sir!" When this secured Edison's attention, he went on: "The State Legislature needs a more humane method than the rope. The search is now on. Firing people from a cannon is clearly a relic of the Crimea. And the guillotine is just too... French. That is why they sent me to you. You have a duty to help me."

"A duty! My only duty is to myself. And that's hard enough to keep. Now leave me alone."

"You won't join with me?"

"Sir, the only thing I would join you in, apart from burning your so-called *findings* in a forge, is in an effort to abolish capital punishment entirely. I have always opposed it, and shall continue to. Good day."

"Then I should take this as a no?"

Edison did not reply.

"Before I am thrown out onto the street, perhaps you could recommend me to some other expert with whom I could speak."

"An expert? Of course, go and talk to Westinghouse if you like. He'll give you the level of third-rate help you seek."

The man looked surprised. "George Westinghouse? Oh no. Oh no, no. No sir. I haven't made myself clear. I couldn't possibly do that. I couldn't go to *him*."

"And why not?"

"Why... because it is with one of Mr Westinghouse's machines that I propose that criminals be electricided."

The inventor stopped. His eyebrows rose. "With a Westinghouse machine?"

The man blinked innocently. "Why yes. With alternating current, which is quite lethal, being transferred at much higher voltages – or so I understand. It is my firm opinion that alternating current is by far the worst danger we face. And I mean to demonstrate this by using one of Mr Westinghouse's machines to perform the ultimate mode of punishment."

The inventor's eyebrows rose even higher. "And your... your *findings* bear this out?"

"Oh yes, they do sir. Definitely. We are currently without a death by AC, but I should not think for long."

"Really? Then... then perhaps I've been too hasty. So... so what else do your findings tell you?"

"Why, that the use of AC must be banned at once. Across the nation. And then the whole world." Brown's eyes blazed with missionary zeal,

and seeing at last the spark of interest in Edison's eyes he was further
delighted when Edison offered him, quite unexpectedly, a cigar. Brown
declined and continued, rising to new heights of self-righteousness.
"You see, I consider myself a philanthropist. And even a murderer
is still a human being. The gallows must become a thing of the past.
The needless suffering of the condemned disgraces all of us. But the
answer escaped me until I became concerned about the dangers of
the alternating current to ordinary people. Suddenly I realized that
the two problems could be solved simultaneously."

"By showing…"

"Yes, that the alternating current is so dangerous that it can, quite
painlessly, dispatch a murderer in the twinkling of an eye! What a
double triumph for civilization that would be."

"Indeed. I'm sure you will find my facilities to your liking."

"Your facilities?"

"I have a new facility. At West Orange. For experiments and development of new ideas. I put it at your disposal. I will help in any
way I can."

"Mr Edison! I'm speechless."

"So tell me. How long do you think it would take you to knock
out this invention?"

"I have no idea. I have a sketch for" – Brown became nervous – "for
an electrical cap. A cap… and shoes. And another for a closet with
an electroplated floor. Another for a saline bath. But I have had no
experience… not as such… in the business of inventing."

Edison pondered these ideas. At his desk he turned to a fresh page
in his journal. "Shoes."

"Shoes," repeated Brown, his words overlapping, half-stealing the
words from Edison's mouth.

"A closet—"

"Closet."

"A ba—"

"Bath!"

"With no restraints? No. The prisoner must be held down, perhaps bound, to a... A bed..."

"Bed! A bed!"

"...would do. A bed... Or a ch—"

"Ch-chair! A chair! A ch-chair!"

"Chair. A very heavy chair. Yes, the criminal should sit. Far more—"

In unison at last, both men erupted with the same word: "Civilized."

"Yes," Edison concluded.

Brown glowed. "Civilized, yes. That was *exactly* what I have been searching for. We're not in the Middle Ages after all."

"Do you have a name for this chair yet?"

"This chair? I... Well you've only just—"

"You will need a convincing name. How about... the" – in thought Edison pinched his bottom lip and then turned his intelligent eyes to Brown – "the West—"

"—inghouse Chair!" Brown exploded, getting there first. "Yes!"

Edison nodded. It was decided. "The Westinghouse Chair."

When Brown had gone, the widower wired a telegram to Morgan on his private telegraph terminal.

JPM STOP URGENT ATTENTION STOP HAVE SOLVED TODAY PROBLEM OF AC VERSUS DC CONTEST STOP HARD AT WORK STOP TAE

* * *

"Mr Edison?"

"Too faint! Louder!"

"Mr—"

In frustration he stamped his boot and repeated: "Louder."

She raised her voice further. "My father, Mr Lewis Miller. He was invited here. By you."

Upon seeing the young woman in the doorway of his West Orange laboratory gripping a half-open parasol, the furrows in the inventor's brow vanished.

"Who? Who are you?"

"He thought – my father thought – you might be interested. In his mower. A motorized machine to cut grass."

He had just been discovered by her looping copper wire three times around his head and then tapping a tuning fork on the edge of a workbench. He made no move to remove the wire or to set down the tuning fork. "I think it," he began, slightly taken with the girl, "I think…" She moved towards him, and he became more than slightly taken with her. "If you…" – she came into the full light thrown by the broad windows – "Yes, I'm certain. It's an astonishing invention. Quite astonishing. I believe it could have… potential. Yes, vast potential actually. Your name?"

"Mina… Mina Miller, sir."

Mina Miller. An olive-skinned beauty of only nineteen, wearing a white dress, her hair combed back and upwards. A slight but constant smile played on her lips.

"Alva Edison, at your service," he bowed his head low, almost an oriental gesture.

"Alva?"

"My first name is Thomas."

"Then why on earth would a Thomas go by Alva? I am sorry if I – before. I didn't mean to interrupt your work. The world needs you to stay hard at work. That's what Pappy says. I was just… looking for…"

"Good. You can help me. Come!"

"Help you?"

"All my muckers – my boys, my men – are in New York. Drinking. Hold these picture cards. Stand six feet away from me, look at each card, and think of the picture that is on each card. I will try and pick up the signal from the etheric realm. Here."

Not at all thinking this curious, she set down her parasol and offered her services. "Of course. I often assist my father in his work. But might I first enquire what it is you are working on?"

Edison attached himself to a battery by means of two wires connected to the copper coil forming a crown on his head. "A machine."

"Which does?"

"It's a… I am trying to invent an apparatus with which we might hear" – he looked into her large, green, innocent eyes – "the dead."

She nodded. "I see. How interesting."

Encouraged by her lack of shock, he added: "I see no reason why, in principle, the dim spirit realm shouldn't be detected by a sensitive enough apparatus." Her eyes were indeed green, indeed large. "It's all to do with magnetism – electricity…"

"What is?"

"We are."

"I see. And so who do you want to talk to? With your apparatus?"

Breaking free of her gaze, he said: "It's a very practical device. The occultists must be denied their monopoly on this subject."

"What do you want to hear them say? The dead?"

But he would not reply to this. "Shall we begin? An apple."

Mina looked back at the card in her hand. She shook her head. "A tree."

"Next card. A…" He closed his eyes in concentration, hoping to commune on those occult channels humanity has always been so tantalizingly close to having access to. "A canoe?"

"A donkey." Her smile deepened. "Perhaps an ass."

"Next." He studied her closely as she turned to the next card. "A house. A house." He closed but then quickly reopened his eyes. "Yes, a house. Definitely a house." But Mina offered only silence. "Not a house?"

"A shoe."

"Next. A... deer."

"No. Just an old" – directing her words at him, enjoying every bit of this exercise – "rather sad-looking... fox."

Edison stared at her. She stared back at him. He took off the copper coil. "Clairvoyance," he said. "It's hard to predict."

"Your device has failed. Good. I believe that electricity and magnetism are the forces of nature by which people who know nothing about electricity and magnetism can explain everything."

"Your father was a good teacher."

"And besides, it would be a terrible calamity to know what the future holds."

" Why?"

"Far better," she replied, "that everything be possible... for as long as possible."

Her smile, at last, drew one from him in return.

* * *

The day was mild. Finches sang in the dogwoods and swooped into the hay barns for nest materials. The new West Orange laboratory that Morgan himself had raised money to see completed had risen quickly out of the landscape, brick by red brick.

Edison was joined by a reporter, who announced he was from the *New York Times*.

"Welcome. Welcome to West Orange. Look around. The first ever self-contained facility for scientific research and development in the world, right here in West Orange."

"An invention factory."

"Exactly. When Menlo Park became too small, we built this."

Something took the reporter's interest. "And what are you inventing over there? All those people with their pets? What are they lining up for?"

Edison turned. "They are... they are..."

A queue of pet owners were lined up outside a door to the main building with their cats, dogs and rabbits. A small fight had broken out among the dogs: their owners gave them short jerks on their leads.

Reporter: "Can we go and take a look?"

Edison reacted sharply. "No. That's – that's the work of another inventor. I know, um, nothing of what they are up to. This facility is for the betterment of science in general. Follow me."

But before Edison could lead the reporter away, a man with a grey-whiskered beagle passed by, complaining loudly: "A quarter for someone's pet? You can't ask people to accept that. Maybe a half-dollar... but I won't part with her for a quarter!"

What Edison did not want the reporter to know was that he had agreed to finance the purchase of two hundred household pets at twenty-five cents apiece as part of Brown's tests on the effects of alternating current on live creatures in those first days of spring. But when the dog pound offered to provide only a half-dozen animals for such "a despicable science", advertisements had to be placed in the local papers, which accounted for the queue of pet owners outside the laboratory door that day, ready, for a small sum, to part with their Rexes, Spots or Cotton Tails.

Ridding himself of the journalist, he buttoned his coat and brushed new dandruff from his shoulders. His stomach was torturing him today. Tobacco tar – or was it guilt about his motherless children, whom he'd badly been neglecting? – as well as the problems of his collapsing businesses, all combined to flood him with acid gastric juices. He slipped past the crowds and entered the new lab.

Even he was shocked by what he saw: an orgy of sorts had broken out. The fifty-cent-a-day girls hired to assemble bulbs were passing around a flagon of green-tinted alcohol used for sealing the vacuums and, one after another, raised the bottle to their lips and drank. It was clear to Edison that there was hardly a girl who wasn't already drunk.

He stepped into the light and roared, "Is it any wonder that we're losing eight cents on every lamp?"

Taking control, he summoned the girls for an inspection and, walking the line, he fired all with green lips; a mere six were innocent, and he congratulated these few for their steadfastness, giving them the morning off while new girls were found to replace the reprobates.

The scene in the chemistry lab was no better. Several dozen boys lay listless and groaning on the floor of the shop. "Good Lord!" Edison shouted.

Hired to make up the chlorine gas that was pumped into the lamp vacuums – a lethal fume if inhaled – Edison first assumed that a disaster had occurred, but seeing that each young man was merely cradling to his chest an open jar of liquid chloroform, the antidote to the poisonous chlorine, it was soon clear that these boys were no better than the girls, and that a general moral lassitude had spread.

"It's like an opium den out there," Edison complained to Charles Batchelor. "This is a *science facility*, not Chinatown."

At Edison's instruction, Batchelor called all the workers together after lunch for an urgent meeting. Standing on an apple box he detailed his new plan: a better bulb. This is what Edison Electric Light must produce now; not one capable of running for two hundred hours, but for two thousand, without burning out.

The workers gasped: "Two thousand hours?"

Edison continued: not only must this bulb reach the market at a cheaper price than its rivals, it must only be able to run on direct current.

None needed an explanation for this last factor: it was a clear strategy to make the best technology in the world available only to those who turned their back on alternating current.

Edison called for a volunteer. "As you know, we have tried to put every possible thing in this country between the armatures of a bulb to try and find the perfect filament. We now need to go farther afield. What I need is a man, one of singular courage, to go to South America to seek out the perfect material for a new filament, a magical fibre in those heavy jungles which when set to light will humble eternity. Scour the rain forests for new materials. The fibre must be fine but strong, to work as a filament *that will run on DC only*. The fate of this laboratory rests on it."

Stirred, one man rose. Tall and willowy, he didn't look robust enough to make a pot of coffee. "I will go. I will do it. If that is what it takes."

"Louder."

"I will go!" The man gave a catarrhal cough. "If that is what it takes!"

"What is your name, sir? You must be new."

"My name is McGowan! Frank McGowan! Started but last week!"

Edison coned his ear. "McGowan, did you say?"

"Yes sir!"

"Are you sound of body?"

"Sound enough I reckon!"

"And a single man too?"

"Single enough now! Wife died last fall!" Cough. "Left me with only myself to think about!" Cough. "So I reckon I'm single now all right!"

He coughed again into a fist. The idea of this man slashing a path through mangrove, inching his way by machete into Peru, was absurd.

"Then you will be more than compensated for your efforts, Frank. The future of this company, and of the lamp itself, will rest now on your shoulders. Now you must all get to work. I have to leave on the next train for New York. I wish you well." The room emptied.

Alone on the station platform he put his hand to his side and winced at the pains just then shooting through him. His traitorous body should be executed for treason.

Batchelor appeared. Joined him on the bench. The softly spoken Brummie from England raised his voice: "There's been trouble ever since we started this new invention of yours. People are behaving quite" – he then placed the focus of the following words upon Edison himself – "out of character. Banners are being posted on the lab doors by someone. Lampoons. We can't find who is doing it. Protesters in town are organizing themselves against these animal experiments. Trouble is brewing."

The inventor rose, began to pace the boards. "Those animals won't feel a thing, I promise you. And remember, in a couple of weeks we'll have done with all this. This whole issue of the currents will be put to rest. Then we'll get on to new things again. Things that'll git us both excited. The most incredible devices – my notebooks are filling up already. Three more weeks, Batch. I promise you. I'll give up New York, and we'll get back to work like before."

Batchelor sighed heavily. "Three weeks?"

"Just to make sure Brown gets off on the right foot, and then that's an end to it. Believe me, I have less of a stomach for his thing than you have."

"Tell me Al – from a scientific point of view – why are you so against this new AC technology? On viability and price it wins hands down.

So instead of spending all our time discrediting it... why don't we just adopt it, take it forward, as we did with the telephone? With the resources we have now it would be easy enough." He gestured about him. It was a simple calculation. "There is room for everyone. And is not the tragic history of the world the story of men impermeable to new ideas, of men locked up in their own self-created realm?"

"You're quoting someone..."

"Oh, just this inventor I once knew."

Edison walked to the window, which allowed a view on his Talking Dolls Workshop where, until recently, eighteen honey-voiced girls had spoken into copper horns, recording nursery rhymes onto tinfoil cylinders to be set into the chests of tin dolls. He had to close that department when the dolls kept arriving in the nurseries of America inexplicably mute.

"I'm taking a few days off, Batch. I want you to handle things while I'm gone. My stomach is bad."

"With all this going on? Where are you going? Back to Wall Street?"

"Chautauqua Lake."

"Fishing?"

"In a manner of speaking."

* * *

"Here you are, Miss Miller."

It was a bright summer's day. With an open parasol, returning from a lakeside walk, Mina crossed the bright-green lawn, her shoes crushing multitudes of wild violets as she approached her guest, who was just then descending the wooden steps from her aunt's house. "We were to take some air an hour ago," she complained at a volume she was still getting used to. "What have you been doing with my family in there?"

131

Sounds of jollity rang from inside the house, and the widower smiled with unusual ease. "Painstakingly orchestrating a string of defeats on the draughtboard at the hands of each of your aunts."

"A sure way to win their favour."

"And by their favour, yours."

"You aim to charm, Mr Edison." She batted her eyes at him.

"Well, the weekend is almost up. I have to get back to West Orange tomorrow, and I'd hoped to declare at least one victory by now."

"How ambitious." Her green eyes moved from him to a premature moon floating just above the treeline.

"But victory has proved elusive."

"Is it your moves that are wrong or is it the strength of the opposition? What an exquisite early moon."

"I suspect both. Let's talk straight. I'm a Michigan farm boy who had a streak of luck and who wishes to share half of it with you."

Her flashing eyes returned to him with fixed focus. "I see. But I have such a crystal-clear picture of the man I will marry – and I am nervous about you."

"And what sort of man is this ghost you have dreamt up as a husband?"

She rumpled her unlined brow. "He must be complicated. That's the first thing. No pimple-faced beau flaunting his father's credentials."

The widower nodded once. "My face is clear of mostly everything but soot and grime and worry... and my father had no credentials to bother anyone except a debt collector."

"A successful older man he needs to be."

"He stands right before you. What's to be nervous about?"

"Someone perhaps thirty-two or even thirty-four, and a man of mystery, a man perhaps rumoured to be seeing a ruthless European adventuress."

"I can lay claim to a certain mystery, but not the lady."

"At the very least a man touched by sadness, so that I can revive him, and with the medicines of youth show him gently how to love again."

"Nurse, oh youthful nurse, you've gone and found your ghost... a heartsick, industrious, mysterious, lucky old ghost." Dramatically, he went down on bended knee.

"But he must not be desperate. I couldn't stand a desperate man."

Edison rose to his feet again and shook his head. "Courting is powerful hard work."

"Let me ask you something... Thomas." She turned her back on him, switching her attentions to something far out in the woods, perhaps something she had seen earlier.

"Alva. I go by—"

"Thomas is much finer."

As the riverboat tooted, she said: "Let me ask you – what level of disrepair are you in? All men are in some measure of disrepair – of what order are you?"

He pondered. "I would say I'm... thirty per cent broken down."

"Thirty?" She nodded. "Normal, then. And what are your abnormalities? In choosing a husband one should try to avoid nasty surprises. Be honest. You are not my only suitor, and a chaperone is not long from appearing."

"I have been a poor father to my three children. They need a mother's love, and that can't easily be counterfeited." What else? He rubbed his chin. It was time for a full disclosure. "I'm deaf. I... I suffer from dandruff. And I sleep badly. And seldom in a bed."

"Deafness... even dandruff can be tolerated. But would a wife be expected to join such a man nightly on his desk or dining table?"

"And I am subject to... visitations. By spirits. But I can never hear what they say. Also, I am currently on a diet of only milk. Six weeks now. I aim to prove the body can exist on a single form of nourishment."

This worried her. "Ah..."

"Oh, and I have twinges."

"I am hardly surprised."

"Of a mental nature. The twinge of ideas, for inventions, ideas superior to any I have ever had. But when I reach out to grasp them, they vanish… unattainable… leaving me just with the trivial bits and bobs that I'll be for ever associated with – an electric pen, a four-way telegraph, the phonograph…"

"And the lamp. Your electric lamp is not trivial. It's miraculous. Only a fine person could invent such a thing."

"Yes. The closest I've come to doing something great. And that's why I won't let it be corrupted, taken over by rogues and cheapened. That's why I'm in the bare-knuckle fight of my life right now."

She turned back to him to deliver her verdict. "Thirty per cent may have been an undervaluation, I must say." Was this her answer? Was she rejecting him? "Any suitor of mine must have a clear conscience. Is your conscience clear, sir?"

"Oh lady. Dear nurse. I am not your ghost after all. Forgive me. I have been wasting your time and mine. A clear… a clear conscience – now that's a luxury I can't afford right now, but… I mean to git it back, and very soon, I promise you that. The pilot light is still burning. And I can always turn the flame back up again. An honest person will always come up doing honest work. So, lady, my Maid of Chautauqua Lake." Here he was referring to the term he had coined in his daily letters to her. "The decision is with you. Wait here on this golden lawn for the perfection of your fantasies to arrive, or… take an old, loving, lovesick widower at his word – that the best in him is not lost for ever."

As far as proposals went, it was the best an old Ohio farm boy could put together. He waited now on her response.

She stared at him in silence, with steady concentration. For an eternity she gave him no reason to hope, nor any reason to walk away.

* * *

The wedding took place on 24th February. Bells rang loudly in Akron, Ohio, calling the notables who had arrived by train from all parts of the country. Under an arch of roses a Methodist minister read the wedding rites, and afterwards the Miller mansion, linked to the church by a long red carpet, reverberated to the sound of an orchestra, while twenty waiters from Chicago served luncheon. The official photographer uncovered his lens many times.

As a present, Thomas gave his wife a new house in Glenmont, New York. Unable to attend, Morgan gifted a fifth-century illuminated missal.

"Can I trust you?" she asked loudly as he steered her backwards in a waltz.

He answered with a kiss on her lips, and then, pressing his mouth close to her ear, delivered the bad news that he would have to cut short the planned two-week honeymoon. "Something has come up in New York that can't wait."

"I see."

"Got a cable this morning from Morgan. I suggest I go on ahead and you follow when you're ready."

"Excuse me?"

"Work."

"And you propose to leave me here?" A steely look had come to her eyes.

He led her from the dance floor. "You have an objection?"

"Sir, I am not a coach to be parked somewhere!"

"Eighty decibels, my love."

"If you have friends, *if* you have friends, then I expect to be introduced to them. If you go to New York, I expect to accompany you. And when – not if – *when* we dine in fine company, I need considerable advance notice. But..."

"My dear? But what?"

"If all you intend to do is work, it is not too late, not too late at all, for me to ask my aunt whether my little old room here in Chautauqua is still available."

With that she was gone, out into the night, her dress washing down the wooden steps into the garden. He ran after her, stopped her in Glendale Cemetery, apologized at length, offered explanations and appeasements until finally, beside the crooked cross of a Civil War soldier, he soothed her with the latest news on the impressive Queen Anne house he was having built for her – where they would, for certain, be happy together. With this her concerns, for the moment, melted, and they moved, arm in arm, back once more towards the gaiety of the party.

* * *

The nut-brown filly was led into the lab's dynamo room. It would be the third and last killing of the day.

"I hear Westinghouse is to sue Edison, and maybe even Morgan as well, in order to defend his name," one New York observer said to another. "If the legislature approves the use of the AC chair powered by his generator, he will sue."

"I hear he is outraged."

"But what of the legal question of whether such a method will be deemed 'cruel and unusual punishment', and therefore against the Eighth Amendment?"

"Well" – a nervous reporter pointed at the stage full of electrical paraphernalia – "it certainly is *unusual*."

"But surely not cruel? Not in the category of burning at the stake."

"Nor crucifixion, it should be said."

"Flogging will continue, I suspect."

"Oh yes, I should hope so. We need that."

"But disembowelling?…"

"No, much too far. But the firing squad will always be an admirable thing, and a staple of the military."

"We haven't mentioned the gallows—"

"The gallows, I think, we must hang on to."

The speaker was interrupted by laughs, as the men of science attached wires to the horse's legs. Only then was a generator wheeled onto the stage with the name Westinghouse ludicrously prominent in raised steel type. One of the men attending it was Thomas Alva Edison, who took his first chance to exit the room and thus avoid all questions.

Outside, the man of science gulped fresh air, hoping to contain his fears, recriminations, his anger, his wife's accusations of moral turpitude – and his lunch.

* * *

"It is war," Westinghouse declared to the press on the steps of the Tribunal. Westinghouse's moustache was tusk-like, the eyes red, the nostrils dilated, the lips pursing with rancour.

"And if this court does not deem Edison's 'chair' cruel and unusual – and thus against the Eighth Amendment – *and* if they continue to use my current in an attempt to smear its good reputation – *then* you will see a war between us the like of which has not been seen before! Gentlemen of the press, you can surely see what's really going on here as well as I do. While my company has orders for 48,000 electric lights in the month of October alone, Mr Edison has sold 44,000 *for the entire year*. What is the public telling him? We know he is hard of hearing, so let me make it loud and clear for him." To much laughter he went on. "I HAVE THE BETTER PRODUCT!" More laughter.

"Yes, but they have more money. So who wins? The *better product* must – it must gentlemen, or else this world is for the dogs! So if he thinks that he and his Wall Street bankers can take a wrecking ball to my business, then, gentlemen, he should henceforth forsake sleep and keep his powder dry!"

He wheeled and mounted the steps at this point like a general, rose to the top of the flight, then wheeled again: "And here's something else for you. I hereby publicly challenge Edison, yes challenge him, to meet me, and in the presence of—"

* * *

Morgan roared with laughter as he read aloud the newspaper report. "'…in the presence of competent electrical experts, take through his body the direct current, while I take through mine an alternating one.'"

In the enamelled stateroom of his floating *Corsair*, Morgan let out a roar. But Edison, seated in silence in the chair opposite, found no pleasure at all in the publicity and not much in the present environment either. Two ladies, whose low-cut bustier left their shoulders bare and precious little to the imagination, had been listening to every word of the article – and the most attractive one, in a red wig, sitting on a corner divan, often met Edison's eyes as she fingered an emerald-green bracelet. It was all that Edison could do to stay in his chair. He ached for oxygen.

"'We will commence with a hundred volts, and we will gradually increase the voltage fifty units at a time until one admits his error.' Let's do it!" The banker lit a cigar. "You'll do it, won't you? That's capital. Capital! Now tell me this, Tom… this electrified chair of yours – is that what you're calling it? – tell me how it will work. People ask me. And I have no idea. Briefly, the theory behind it. How will it, you know" – he blew out the match – "dispatch a man?" He sent out a shot of smoke between them. "You realize, of course... if it doesn't kill anyone, we're finished. The public will go the way of the frontrunner in this battle. We need AC to kill the first criminal in the blink of an eye. Nothing less than the blink of an eye. After that, who will want AC in their home?"

Edison nodded. It was all true. The stakes couldn't be higher. The chair had to be lethal. "I want to end this."

"So do I."

"No. I want to call it quits."

"Tom – I have more money sunk into you than I care to reveal to myself. Remember what we are building here together."

"Remind me."

"Remember that we have, in this incandescent lamp, a product that everyone on this planet will eventually seek to acquire. Your invention. Your name. Was there ever such a product in the history of commerce? As indispensable as fire, air, water. The first element that we can put a price tag on. One day you'll be bigger than the government." The moustache twitched as he grinned. In a burst of amorousness the banker then grabbed the wrist of his redhead lover, pulling her back down onto his lap. Edison thought the conversation was over, but while the banker seemed to be absorbed in kissing her neck in short puckered smacks, he was still able to ask: "Now explain to me what AC is. At the moment... people are still confused. Is electricity safe or is it not?... DC or AC? Gas or electricity?... And tell me more about this Serb..."

"Tesla."

"Exactly." Then, to his lover: "You taste so sweet I could eat you."

"He's mad. Tesla."

"Marvellous news." Morgan continued to kiss his lover.

"I heard," Edison ventured further, turning his eyes from the love-making, "he recently even had his testicles removed."

This idea made Morgan break off his kisses. "Is that true? His testicles?"

"So as to… I'm told… so as to make himself a better receptor for divine messages."

"I had no idea testicles could be an impediment. Did you?"

Edison could only shrug.

"Anyway, balls or not, he's doing a lot of damage to us with these demonstrations. How in hell is he able to withstand 250,000 volts at a time? You tell me you're killing horses in West Orange with – what? – with 700 volts? So how can he take 250,000 into himself? I'm confused. And I'm worried. Tesla is extraordinary, but surely not miraculous."

Morgan's luscious redhead – her uplifted bosom tickled by his moustache and the gentle brushing of his nose – giggled and brought a goblet to his mouth.

Edison relayed the theory in the simplest layman's terms. The voltage was a red herring. Brown was a fool for prattling on about it in the papers. No, the *frequency* of the alternation was the deadly thing: it was the *hertz* that killed you.

"You've lost me entirely," Morgan said. "I'm not sure I want you to go on."

Edison persisted, even though Morgan did not seem to be listening any more. "The current Tesla is using for his demonstration is a piece of trickery. It's not the same quality of current his generators provide in Greensburg. A mere 700 volts of *that* would kill you in seconds. No, for the stage he's developed a step-down transformer, that cleverly adjusts both dangerous elements in his current, the hertz and the amperage, so that it's harmless, while allowing the voltage to be astronomic."

"I'm not sure," Morgan muttered, as his nose and moustache elicited another giggle, "it's worth going any further."

"Oh, it's quite simple. All electricity comprises three parts. The first is called volts. This is the force that the current is pushed out at by the generator. Second is the hertz. All electricity alternates in its natural state when generated: it cycles back and forth. Tesla knows that when a human being receives an electrical shock, pain is felt only as the current alternates or changes direction: the more alternations per second, or hertz, the greater the pain. He discovered that, just as the human ear cannot sense a blast from a dog whistle or any sounds above a certain frequency, at some mysterious point – at about 700 hertz cycles per second – the pain signals, the *alternations* – come too rapidly to be felt any longer, and so AC become painless." Edison said this with a sigh of resignation. "The third thing is amperage, the *amount* of current. His stage transformer also lowers the amperage to almost nothing, which reduces the heat produced, ensuring that his body doesn't burn up. So the voltage can run into the thousands. It's quite brilliant. Spectacular. And there's just enough amperage there to power that single bulb he holds up. But not a city: for that he needs to raise the amps and hertz back to where they're dangerous."

Amperage, transformer, frequency, voltage, hertz? Morgan tried to process these terms as best he could with a perfumed whore on his lap, but only one question arose in him: "So are people dying in Greensburg, Pennsylvania, then? They'd better be."

"Not as many as I would have expected."

"So he's invented a better product? This is what you're saying?"

"No. I believe DC is safer."

"This is what you *believe*? Well, I hope we find *proof*. You sounded like his publicist just now."

Edison was taken aback. "I was just describing, in purely scientific terms—"

"Well, I suggest you find less flattering terms when you next describe his system to anyone."

141

Edison shifted in his seat. He really wished to be gone. "His current is a killer. Make no mistake about it. And the man is a lunatic."

"That's more like it." Morgan finally pushed his woman off him, both hands on her buttocks, and turned back to Edison. "I was beginning to get worried about you. If I'm backing the wrong horse, tell me now."

Edison paused before replying. "At 700 volts, without a transformer, I assure you, alternating current is lethal. And we'll be employing *1,500* volts of his current on the chair. Tesla is a maniac. He has to be stopped."

Holding a searching look Morgan moved on. "Good. Let's do that. And then let us electrify earth, heaven and, if needs be, hell. On second thought, Westinghouse can have the contract for hell." Morgan straightened his clothes.

"Alva, I want to discuss amalgamating Edison Electric Light and all your manufacturing concerns into one giant combination. How about: Edison General Electric? If you approve, it will be capitalized at a value of twelve million dollars. I'll take half the shares. In return, you'll have all the money you'll ever need. A royalty plus stock. You'll be a rich man."

"I thought... you'd lost faith in me."

"Lost faith? Certainly not. You're my best invention."

The listless redhead, now with a bottle of Pommery, rose to refill Morgan's hovering glass. With an indolent look and a nod at Edison, she left the room, following her friend. The inventor's heart jumped as her eyes swept across him, and when Morgan saw this exchange he slipped from his pocket a small silver case no bigger than a watch face. "By the way, Alva, take your pick. There are a dozen private rooms on board. I think you are taken with that redhead. A fine choice, I must say. And don't worry. I have here the latest mark of progress." He drew from the case a most curious item: organic and shrivelled. "More vital in the hotter climes, where the ladies sweat and dare not wash, but they also solve a lot of problems here."

"What is it?"

On Morgan's open palm lay the skin of a tiny snake. "Isn't it extraordinary? You talk of real progress? Here is the latest thing. Vulcanized rubber. Whatever will they think of next? Excuse me, I mean, what will *your sort* think of next?" He pushed the repugnant object closer to Edison's face. "Dulls the pleasure somewhat, but far superior to the fish membranes of my youth. That smell was" – he sniffed nostalgically – "shall we say, detrimental to romance. Take one. Keep it. It's a gift. It's even washable."

Understanding its function and, more to the point, its second-hand nature, Edison waved it away. "No, no. I am a married man."

"Then here. Take two."

* * *

Mina stood at the window of her new house in Glenmont.

Her plans for a perfect marriage, hatched on the long, aquatint afternoons of her youth, for a perfect marriage had dramatically failed.

At the window she wondered by what act of witchcraft such an ardent suitor had turned, so quickly, into such an elusive husband.

The new garden was in full bloom, but already she anticipated frost.

As a new wife she had all the usual concerns of a woman who marries a complete stranger, but she now had to add to these the knowledge that his new workshops were a scene of barbaric practices.

Also, he had all but stopped talking to her. Even on the swing seat on her porch during the brief courtship, when he had been at his most passionate, she had known she was marrying a *sourd* but she had never bargained on a *muet* as well. Since their honeymoon – and

143

even then he seemed to be in a rush, as if late for some more pressing appointment – his one romantic gesture had been to invite her to a dinner in his honour at the New York Telegrapher's Union.

Her hopes had risen. From New York, where he was tied up with work, he wrote and spoke of being a better husband "this time around". Flowers arrived. Was the glamour she craved finally about to arrive as well?

She bought a new dress on Madison Avenue, took out her wedding diamonds, made herself up. But at the grand dinner a telegraph key sat beside each place setting, and during the entire evening all communication between guests was restricted to telegrams!

She looked hopelessly at her husband, but saw that he was in a world that suited him in every way.

At the head table, the only woman in an entire hall of black-suited male telegraphers, she was too stunned to defy the rules and so remained a statue in that echo chamber occupied by a thousand crickets, watching aghast as people sent cables to others within speaking range. An hour passed. Finally, she cried, then grew angry. With no understanding of Morse code, and wondering to what unearthly planet she had been transported, she blew her nose into a handkerchief of *point d'Alençon*, then shouted to the room: "What exceptional weather we are enjoying this fall!"

The entire gathering froze, stared at her. Her husband excused them both. He put her on a carriage. Before closing the carriage door he told her he was sorry if she was finding this testing, but his was no ordinary life. He only hoped that she would soon adjust and somehow find a way to love him, despite the difficulties of his character. "I love you very much. Never doubt that, Deary."

* * *

Mina, at her bedroom window, decided to give herself one more month before leaving him. A one-month trial, then, and if he continued to give priority to his work to the exclusion of both her and his children, she would divorce and return home to her beloved family in Chautauqua. She wasn't afraid of divorce. But she wouldn't give up on him just yet: her adolescent hopes had not quite died, and in theory he might still be suitable for her.

While deep in such thoughts, Margarita came in and presented her with two dozen roses. "Who are these from?" Mina asked.

"Your husband."

"In the absence of a man, flowers."

But hardly had she said this than the man in question appeared in the doorway, carrying an even larger bunch. When he saw that she was angry, he said: "What is the matter? You don't like red roses?"

Mina picked up the *New York Times* and read aloud: "'*The dog stood in the lattice box, the wires around him led...*'"

"I would rather discuss poetry later."

"'*He knew not that electric shocks so soon would strike him dead...*'"

"Mina. I came here to—"

"'*At last there came a deadly bolt. The dog, O where was he?*'"

"Please... Mina..."

Mina put down the paper. Edison sighed, but he did so too soon, as Mina had committed the last line to memory. "'*Three hundred alternating volts had burst his viscera.*'"

Edison sat on a footstool. She stared at him and was pleased, at least, that he was feeling something. "Thomas, they say you are killing—"

"STOP! Please." He rose again. "I must be going. Work to do." He paused at the door. "Um... Your new dress looks very handsome."

"It's not new. And you look awful."

"Do I?"

"Ill. Are you sleeping?"

"I must go. We'll take a holiday soon. Florida, I promise. Or Saratoga Springs. We'll take the waters."

He left her.

That night he did not reappear.

Unable to sleep, she climbed the stairs to the attic, carrying an oil lamp. She knocked on the small door of Margarita Sanabria.

The maid blanched at letting the lady of the house into her small, untidy room. "Señora?"

"Do you mind if I come in?"

Inside there was only room for a single bed and a night table. Wild flowers sat on the table. A crucifix hung on the wall.

"You've made it nice."

"Señora?"

"I want to ask you about Mr Edison's first wife."

"Señora?"

"You were her personal maid for many years. What was she like? I need to know about her. Thomas has told me so little."

"Mrs Mary? Oh, she was very nice."

"Anything else? Tell me more. Much more."

But the maid did not oblige. She only said:

"Mr Edison loves you very much."

Mina looked up, startled by the maid's words. "Do you think so? I can't help feeling he sees... only Mary. Everywhere. I wonder if it was a love that can never be matched? I feel as... as if I am competing with a ghost."

"Señora," the maid shook her head. "Some of the things you ask can never be known by the living. And others, only a wife can learn."

Mina prepared to go. "I don't know how to read him, that's all. His moods. Could Mary reach him?"

"Read him? Understand him? Oh yes. They had their system."

Mina's eyes widened in sudden interest. "System?"

"Morse," the maid replied. "The code. Morse Code. You must learn the code. The tap-tap-tap. Mr Edison and Mary, they had Morse Code. And you must too."

* * *

Under cover of darkness the four orang-utans were offloaded at the West Orange railway station and in three unmarked boxes taken by horse and dray to the laboratory.

Governor David Hill of New York had his sights set firmly on the presidency. Convinced of his need to associate himself with forward-thinkers, he had journeyed a great distance to join a select group of Edison employees as the tarpaulins were removed.

"My God!" the Governor stammered.

He had never seen an orang-utan before, let alone two giant ones and two babies up close. The adults were mighty creatures. Each possessed the strength of ten men. Their high-crowned foreheads had the hue of basalt; their monumental heads would, if hollowed out and upturned, surely hold five gallons. Their bloodshot eyes carried intelligence and drifted slowly under thick, sculptured lids. "What creatures," the dignitary said.

The dispirited primates had been captured in Siam, then shipped directly to West Orange for this secret experiment, one which Harold Brown hoped would be the definitive test. These creatures possessed all the vital attributes of a criminal – size, physiology, strength, cunning – but where they were of superior value right now was their inability to write letters of protest to the *New York Times*.

There was little patience among the staff. Harold Brown barked orders, eager to impress the Governor. Meanwhile, Batchelor approached Edison to speak of his reservations one last time. But the inventor waved his colleague aside. No one, Edison pointed out, would take the least pleasure in this, but state legislatures were wavering in the face of hysterical editorials which questioned the morality of electrocution. As a result, positive proofs must be given to the lawmakers that the chair could work on a human being without causing any horrible incidents. Edison was simply not in a position to grant the reprieve Batchelor sought.

"Batch, the best thing we can do for these animals is to git this God-awful thing over with as fast as possible." The inventor looked ashen himself, strained, ready to snap. His hand sat on his stomach. "Please," Edison whispered, as if asking for pity, "don't make a scene today."

And so the male ape was selected to go first. He was isolated, separated from his family. This great kingly specimen made little effort to resist the attachment of wires and restraints to his legs and arms. Despite his incredible strength, he made it easy for the staff to reach inside the bars, part the coat hairs thicker than a horse's, find the flesh, the bone, attach the copper plates and then, as if on familiar terms with him, to pat and caress his heavy limbs, stroke the colossal feet and the hunched back. Was he bewildered? Was he experiencing what humans call a depression? A nickname was even coined: "Brutus". It seemed to befit his heroic bearing. And what of his animal thoughts? Francis Upton, standing back and watching the process, shook his head from side to side. At the risk of being shouted down, he approached his boss one last time with a question. As a creature born free of man, whose last impression of the world would be of scientists, white-coated and workmanlike in their death preparations, what might this ape's verdict be on this attempt at progress? Batchelor begged his boss to reconsider.

Edison's nervous reply only returned them to their earlier debate. "You think I don't feel the same? But just imagine if alternating current is allowed to proliferate. *Think...* of the loss of *human* life farther down the track. Do you want *that* on your conscience, all those other deaths, when you could have done something? We have to push ourselves to the limits. And we have no choice but to conduct business on the level of our competitors."

The ape was now ready. In a last act of sentimentality, the technicians drew again the tarpaulins over the other cages so that his family would be spared the sight of his ordeal. Some wanted the cages taken away completely, but the movers were taking their supper and, besides, the animals weighed a ton.

Batchelor gave the task of throwing the switch to a young boy, a shaky apprentice. On cue the lad muscled a lever. The current flowed the short distance into the animal. All eyes swung to the ape, who yelped once before going into a silent spasm: Brutus looked as if he were trying to loosen himself from his own skin.

"Stop," Edison shouted. The current was cut. "Too slow. Much too slow. Check there's no belt drive slippage on the dynamo and send down 1,000 volts. Quickly!"

Brown did not contest this and the current flowed again.

This time it became clear that the wires had not been properly attached to the ape, for its coat burst into flames. It reminded Upton of a brush fire that sweeps in a high wind on an arid hill. Barely held by its straps, Brutus pounded at his own skin, tossed, struggled, screaming his outrage as the flames threatened his head. But it was no good. He was ablaze.

"Put him out, put him out!" the onlookers shouted.

But this wasn't simply done. No fire buckets were on hand. No one had expected such an outcome. Besides, inside its cage the animal was unapproachable, beyond help.

Acting instinctively, Edison and three technicians hauled the tarp back over the cage in an effort to cut off the oxygen and stifle the blaze. But the unbearable screams did not subside even then. The audience turned away, convinced that they were hearing an outcry from hell.

After five minutes the noise stopped. Edison asked for the tarpaulin to be lowered. The great beast was lying on his back, eyes closed, with smoky patches of his skin exposed, singed hair encircling smouldering meat.

Edison's eyes shifted to the Governor, and the two men exchanged a look of revulsion. Edison shook his head in grim apology. The Governor was about to be sick: his hand came to his mouth.

Batchelor meanwhile pulled off his gloves and angrily unbuttoned his smock. He was shouting, but perhaps only to himself: "I'm taking no more! No more! This is… this is an abomination!"

Edison weakly took his employee's arm, lowered his voice to a whisper. "I beg you, Batch, don't leave now. This is the *last*… god-damn it! No more after tonight, I promise. I promise you."

"The last? *Is* it the last?"

"I promise."

But Batch was beyond being soothed. He shook loose Edison's grip and walked off, watched by his friend. Edison couldn't blame him. Wouldn't he like to walk away himself?

Governor Hill needed air, and was led outside. While he was gone, the technical staff once again attached wires to the suffering animal. With a current of seventy amps his magnificent life was finally snuffed out. And then came the turn of the female.

THOMAS

"Sir?"

"What is it?"

"You were shouting. Talking to someone."

"Talking to…"

"You were talking to someone. Just now."

The young boy had just returned to the train platform from a short visit behind some nearby bushes and had been alarmed to see the old man shouting and waving his stick.

The old man lifted his chin. "Was I? Never… well I… never you mind. Never you mind. What's your name?"

"Winthrop."

"Winthrop?" Thomas studied the young man, then finally nodded, taking him at his word. "Winthrop. Alright. What time… train… should be here any second."

"Are you all right, sir?"

"Do I look all right?" His eyes fell to Winthrop's hand. "What are you *doing*?"

"Smoking, sir." In Winthrop's hand there was a cigarette.

"Put it out. Out at once!"

"But you chew tobacco, sir?"

"Tobacco ain't harmful. At least, not after a man is fully formed. But the use of paper and tobacco together, in the form of cigarettes, is extremely harmful and causes degeneration."

"Degeneration?"

"Affects the moral sense. Only degenerates who have retrogressed to the lower animal orders smoke cigarettes."

After a moment, the boy looked at the cigarette in his hand, then quickly ground it out under his foot. "I didn't know that," he said.

But then the old man's eyes widened. He cocked his head. "Do you hear it, son?" Once more he checked his findings by bending over and biting on the handle of his stick. After several more seconds of closed-eye concentration, he said:

"Full head of steam from the west." He pointed his cane towards Dearborn.

The boy looked up the track, sceptical. He saw it as his duty now, rather than to bring the old man back to this earth, to humour him on these forays into incomprehensibility. "Yes sir." But this time the smoke of an engine actually did become visible. "Well I'll be," he said, amazed.

When the old man moved to the edge of the platform, Winthrop did the same.

The advancing train, which would have taken the boy in the wrong direction, grew in size and sound, but it soon became clear that it was not going to stop at all. It roared past them as they stood there, and its only effect was to ruffle their hair. When it was gone, the old man spoke first.

"Brakes not working."

"You think so?"

"Blame George Westinghouse for that."

Winthrop looked puzzled. "George Westinghouse? The refrigerator man?"

"Invented the locomotive air brake. Never worked worth a darn. I told him so too."

The boy was impressed. "Did you know him, sir?"

The old man looked aggrieved. "Westinghouse? Yes. I knew him."

The boy then recalled a detail from his schooling. "Didn't he come up with the current? Didn't he invent electric power?"

The old man spun and shot him a look of serious fury, lifting his cane like a sword. "How do you know about that?"

The boy drew back. "School, sir. I learnt it in school is all."

"In school? Then your master should be shot! They're teaching that in school now, are they?" But quickly the old man sighed and sagged again. "Teaching that in school…" He shouldn't excite himself. His strengths were limited. And the year was 1929, after all, not 1888.

"Sir? Are you OK?"

"Tesla."

"Sir?"

"The Devil and Nikola Tesla."

"Shall I get a doctor, sir?"

"The Devil himself."

EDISON

A single wooden chair awaited him. A sturdy chair built of timbers long and slow in growing. Into it sat Thomas Alva Edison, called to the stand by the clerk in the hearing convened to establish whether an electric chair is against the Constitution. The famous inventor looked to all to be extremely uncomfortable and gloomy.

Questioning him was Mr W.B. Cockran. Shrewd, restless, the man was said to be the best orator in America, and he laid the foundations of his argument with his first question:

COCKRAN: Mr Edison. I understand that you are an expert in the immutable nature and boggling metaphysics of electricity?
EDISON: I can't hear you. You gotta speak up.
COCKRAN: Forgive me. You are an expert in the field of electricity?

Sensing dangers, a barb to every question, Edison responded warily.

EDISON: I've spent... twenty-six years in the perfecting of electrical inventions, but one always remains an apprentice.
COCKRAN: And what a list of inventions! The phonograph. The incandescent lamp – or is that one still being contested?
EDISON: You'd better ask the patent office.
(Gallery laughter)

155

COCKRAN: The stock-ticker. The four-way telegraph. An improved telephone. Oh, and the electric canoe! *(To the gallery)* To electrify a canoe! *(The gallery laughs harder)* Marvellous. And now – a chair. A new kind of chair.

Already at a disadvantage, Edison's heart sank. This would be a far greater ordeal than he'd feared. His hands tightened their grip on the arms of the wooden chair, and tension filled his limbs.

EDISON: It is not my chair.
COCKRAN: Then whose chair is it?
EDISON: Mr Brown's. Harold Brown.
COCKRAN: Ah. But you *are* the author of this pamphlet, are you not? *(Holds up a booklet)* Title? 'A Warning'.
EDISON: I am not the author of that.
COCKRAN: 'A Warning' is distributed by your company?
EDISON: Perhaps.
COCKRAN: It warns, does it not, of the *dangers*... inherent... in the *alternating current* – or, as the author calls it, quote, "the executioner's current".
EDISON: My views on this issue are well known.
COCKRAN: Indeed, one need only read this booklet, one feels, to learn them exactly! *(Titters in the crowd)* So please tell us – why are you involved in such an aggressive propaganda campaign against Mr Westinghouse at this time?
EDISON: My company is opposed to the proliferation of the science he advances.
COCKRAN: Purely a technical objection then? A scientific one?
EDISON: Yes.
COCKRAN: Nothing to do with business. And the fact that Mr Brown works at your laboratory – on a chair to kill prisoners – which

will run on Mr Westinghouse's "executioner's current" – a chair which is being *named* after my client – and is therefore dripping with negative publicity – and which, if it should work quickly on a human being will make my client's name *synonymous* with instant death – all pure coincidence?

(Edison does not reply)

COCKRAN: Here is my recapitulation. The great inventor of light, the maker of – *an electric canoe*! *(Titters)* – the man who put an orchestra in a box so that every household can hear rhapsodies at the crank of a handle, a humanist par excellence… is it possible that such a man is now exterminating cats, dogs, horses – some say two adult orang-utans! – in preparation for his first human being, all out of purely scientific interest?

(Edison does not reply)

COCKRAN: Tell us – what does an electrical shock feel like?

EDISON: I wouldn't know. I've never had one.

COCKRAN: You've never had one? Never?

EDISON: No.

COCKRAN: To never have experienced the material of one's profession seems an astonishing level of ignorance. *(Mumbling from the gallery)* Truly, this is no less strange to me than hearing of a sailor, his whole life on the oceans, who has never once dipped his hand in the water!

(The Clerk demands the gallery be silent)

EDISON: I can't hear you. I can't hear you. I said I can't hear what you're saying. Speak up!

WOMAN'S VOICE: Murderer!

(Edison jolts in his chair)

COCKRAN: An astonishing level of ignorance.

WOMAN'S VOICE: Murderer!

* * *

Morgan read of how the man, the killer, struck his wife with a hatchet repeatedly, then ran into the Buffalo night. Morgan set the newspaper aside and took a long medicinal puff on his fifth cigar of the morning. The story which had curled his intestines ran under the headline: "ELECTRIC CHAIR RULED NEITHER CRUEL NOR UNUSUAL... KEMMLER CLEARED TO DIE!"

William Kemmler – what kind of man was this wretch? The story said he had murdered his wife after becoming jealous that she was seeing another man. So now, then, Kemmler must also die. By electric current. Experimentally.

Feeling unwell, Morgan cancelled his meetings for the rest of the day. He returned to his brownstone on Madison Avenue with a migraine and urgently summoned Reverend Rainsford of St George's Episcopal Church.

The butler showed the Reverend straight into the study, where Morgan waited with the drapes drawn and with his head in his hands.

"Thank you for coming, Reverend," moaned the banker, as the butler asked: "Will there be anything else, sir?"

Morgan, bent over, shook his large heavy head, and the butler sealed the door on the banker and the clergyman, returning at intervals to listen at the door, as was the protocol of the house, but heard only the muted sounds of confession and finally the not-unfamiliar sound of Mr Morgan weeping.

* * *

And then milk appeared. The tray startled him. He leapt in fright, knocked it over. Milk swept over the notebooks, broken glass ricocheted across the floor. Mina apologized. She'd only been trying to make him happy on his first night back in their new home in two weeks.

She sat down miserably in one of his leather armchairs in his study as Edison called for Margarita to come in and clear up. When the maid was done, Mina offered, in a conciliatory vein: "It's good at least to see you are inventing again."

He didn't look up. "No. I'm merely attempting to do that."

"Come to bed."

"I can't. Not right now."

"Do you mind if I... if I just sit here and watch the fire? I am feeling very lonely tonight."

Still he didn't raise his head from his notebook – where, she noticed, his pen did more rapid crossing-out than new work. "It'll be very boring for you," he finally said.

She folded her hands on her knees, sighed and then watched a log in the fireplace become wrapped in flame. "Did you see—"

"Mina!"

"Yes, deary?"

"*Please!*"

She smoothed the multiple layers of her dress, refolded her hands and regarded her wedding ring for some time. "Oh, while I remember it, the lights in the bedroom aren't working right."

"They... Ts!... Mina, I used them this morning. They work perfectly."

"No. They're buzzing. Truly. You can't hear them, but I can. I am too scared to use them."

"You're imagining it."

"You mean the buzzing is in my head then?"

"That's a question for Doctor Phillips."

Her face flushed as he flipped to a new page, as if abandoning a brilliant prototype: what was it he was working on, she wondered

– perhaps a carrier of people to the moon, or to the bottom of the sea... a contraption the world would never see because of her interruption?

She bit her tongue, but soon felt the need to be heard once more.

"You must eat."

"No food. I told you. Just milk."

"These milk diets. You are not old enough to become truly eccentric."

"Man can live on a single complete source of nourishment. We are nursed on milk alone, and are never stronger."

"Oh," she said, just remembering the letter that had come for him, drawing it from the pocket of her dress. He opened it and read it.

"What does it say?"

"Nothing," he replied.

"A letter to you is now a letter to both of us."

He handed it to her. She read aloud: "Dear Mr Edison... urgent... need you... Auburn Prison... the chair is now ready and—" She broke off. "You are going to proceed with this? What is happening to you?"

"Happening? I'm suffering from an atrophy – a paralysis of curiosity. I can't create. Can't invent. Can't imagine. Can't work. Trying to be a businessman has had a disastrous effect on me. It's destroyed my talent."

"And how many more things will you let it destroy?"

"Mina—"

"You are an inventor. You once told me that your religion was to do good. Do you remember? You said you were in 'the improvement game'. And such a man, the man I married, is now going to solve a problem by killing someone? Is this how we solve things now, Thomas?"

"It's better than the rope."

"Why does he have to be killed at all?"

"Because—"

"Can he kill again from his lonely prison cell?"

"Look, it's going to be painless."

"How do *you* know? You don't know. Do you? In your testimony you said you had never suffered an electrical shock. How do you know what it will feel like to die with a streetful of electricity in your veins?"

When he did not respond, she snatched a fork off the tray and started to tap, steel on steel, a message. Her first telegram.

"What are you doing?" His face showed shock, displeasure.

On she tapped. Concentrating deeply.

"That's not right!" he shouted. "Where did you—"

And as she continued to send her message, he grabbed her Morse-sending hand. "Stop! Mina... if you love me... leave... me... be!"

She obeyed and flew from the room.

What is happening to me? he asked himself. *The world is my country, to do good my religion.* But in the service of good, was he still? Tom Paine was an idealist, a pamphleteer who died despised on two continents by royalists and revolutionists alike – an impoverished drunk. Even his bones were lost by those devotees assigned to protect them. And Faraday, his other hero, turning down knighthoods and clinging to his principles? He lived in the celestial bubble of his theories and never once had to sit for lunch at Delmonico's with aggressive millionaires who offered him the world: was he to be emulated?

His eyes had turned to the electric light, the object of all his woes. Were the lights truly playing up, as Mina said? He rose and went to the nearest one, set into a converted gas sconce on the wall. What were Cockran's words? "An astonishing level of ignorance." A sailor indeed he was – his whole life on the oceans, but never once dipping his hand in the water. And into this "water" a man would soon be plunged. Well, what was the nature of this water? What was the sensation when human flesh and bone, and not metal, were the conductor? Staring at the bulb, he rolled up his sleeve and, using the edge of a nearby curtain as a cloth, screwed out the lamp without turning off the switch. "An astonishing…" – slowly, deliberately, he moved his free hand towards the fixture – "level of…" until, speaking aloud the word "ignorance", gripped the lamp stand hard, pressing his thumb down on the terminals inside.

He was thrown backwards, convulsed with the equivalent pain of having every nerve in his body filed with a rasp at the same time. Also, he was thrown into such a sudden mental darkness that his legs gave out and he found himself on his back with his limbs quivering, eyes unable to focus on anything until the chandeliers above him became clear again.

After some minutes he got back to his feet and, ignorant of electricity no longer, he returned to his desk, where he closed the notebook in which he'd been scribbling random ideas. In eight steps he crossed the room and cast the book into the grate, whereupon the fire – voracious reader – started to turn the pages, revealing them to contain not a single decent invention.

* * *

Thomas Alva Edison was quietly admitted into Auburn prison on a lowering early-August afternoon.

As much as he regretted this whole affair, he had a sudden need to see first-hand the conditions under which his bastard invention would be used. He followed the strangely shoeless warden towards the cell of the murderer condemned to die by electrical current.

He passed by tourists buying entrance tickets for the cell-block tour. Pausing at the ticket booth himself, he noted you could either buy a single ticket to let you peep through spy holes at the prisoners in the cells, or you could buy a double pass, which would allow you to take in Niagara Falls on the same day. The "Prison-Waterfall Day Out" was a popular hit. The queue was long. He shook his head in consternation.

The flagstone passageways between the inner and outer skins of the prison walls were so narrow that Edison had to rotate his shoulders slightly as he passed. The interior walls were dotted with pinpoints of light, tiny perforations at viewing height. He walked by the many tourists already with their faces pressed to the cold damp stone spying on the criminals in their natural habitat. A bizarre amusement. How strange to pay two dimes to remind yourself what a blessing freedom was.

Edison had asked to be taken directly to Kemmler's cell, but even he couldn't resist stopping at one of the many radiant peepholes along the way.

He put his own eye to a hole. Inside, an elderly man in a striped suit sat against the far wall, his legs drawn up, his head lowered on his knees in a posture of defeat. Edison felt a surge of pity. It was impossible to know whether he was a maniac or just a badly defended innocent. The state of legal defence for the poor ranged from bad to non-existent. What a fate this would be for an innocent man. Could he himself withstand it for a single day if he were to be thrown in here? He thought of the scientific heretics of history, condemned for theories or discoveries deemed criminal, who refused to recant or deny their pure ideologies. He felt vividly now the price such people had paid for ethical bravery. And how did he rate against such men by comparison? Where was he, next to a Galileo or a Giordano Bruno?

Ashamed, he hurried on, his head lowered, learning en route the mystery of the jailer's footwear. All the staff wore no shoes so as better to listen out for shouts, gurgles, screams, the scrape of a file perhaps – all of which had to be heard at once if a killing, an escape, a suicide was to be prevented.

The warden had stopped and was pointing at one shining hole, isolated from the rest. This must be it. Edison set his palms on the damp stone and moved his eye to the light. An animated drama at once presented itself.

Inside was a man in his late forties, very thin, of unremarkable appearance, but with an immaculate beard, a narrow neck, almost a dandy despite the regulation clothes. The now famous villain – the cartoonists had made his looks known to the public – lay on a thin bed, calmly considering his situation, staring at the ceiling, wide awake. But – Edison could not help wondering – thinking about what? About electricity perhaps?

Kemmler was locked into a space no more than one body length long, one body length high and only half a body length wide, and the inventor was struck by the living hell created to punish him. Insanity would be hard to keep at bay here. The warden leant in to whisper that Kemmler had been in solitary isolation like this for fifteen months, permitted to speak only occasionally with a member of the press for most of the time. Whether this last leniency qualified as human contact was debatable, and Edison surprised himself with the consoling thought that in such horrible circumstances his chair might prove a welcome mercy.

"Does he know that he is to be the first?" he asked.

"To use the chair? Oh yes. And he is not afraid. Not since he learnt that Mr Thomas Edison himself was behind its manufacture."

"You should not have told him that."

"Why? Is it not true?"

"It is the Westinghouse system. It has nothing to do with me."

The warden smiled, knowingly. "Still, he speaks very highly of you. In fact, sir, it was all we could do to stop him from writing you a note of thanks."

"You can't be serious?"

"He believes your name guarantees him a speedy departure. He holds you in huge esteem."

"Then you must tell him he is mistaken. You must tell him. The chair is the work of the New York State Legislature alone."

"But surely… surely you would not deny him this single comfort?"

"Yes, I would. I do not want the last name on his mind as he leaves this earth to be mine. Promise me you will tell him it has nothing to do with me."

"Very well."

Regaining his composure, Edison reflected: so it is pain, the anticipation of it, which preoccupies this prisoner day after endless day. And, poor fool, in an attempt to minimize the prospect of it, he is ready to embrace even those complicit in his death. How much pain did he anticipate he would suffer? Five seconds of it? Ten seconds? Had all his earthly hopes been reduced to this single question?

At intervals Kemmler raised one hand, then the other, fanning his fingers to examine them, as women will do when trying on a ring in a jewellery store. And no sooner did he lay his hands down at his sides than up again came one hand or the other. Another examination followed. It was a nervous routine, one that in recent months had probably become obsessive.

"What is he doing?" Edison queried.

The warden took over at the hole. "Oh. That. His fingernails. Yes. We call him 'The Gent' actually. Keeps asking for a nail file, a penknife. But these are obviously restricted items. And so he grooms them by whatever means he finds. All he does all day. Look now. Quick." He gave Edison back his place.

Edison reset his eye. Kemmler was dragging a fingernail back and forth against the stone wall, buffing its edge to perfection. For whom did he imagine he was keeping up his looks? What use were the nails of a Louis XVI in the hell of a New York jail?

The warden's breath blew humid on Edison's ear. "You see? Vanity. Even on the walk to the gallows they wish for a mirror. To tweak a moustache, brush back hair, straighten a collar. Outward order, a substitute for inward peace. I really wish they wouldn't ask. It makes my job so much more disagreeable to have to dispatch a murderer in the guise of a gentleman."

Kemmler was either unaware of the eyes at the hole or was unaffected by them. Since each prisoner knew of his exotic role in the local tourist industry, he might have been expected to glance from time to time in the direction of the peephole, bark out words offensive enough to win a short withdrawal of the curious eye. But in this particular dungeon, there was a prisoner so absorbed in his manicure, so desperate to distract his mind from his fate, that he was immune to any sightseer.

Or so it seemed to Edison, until the prisoner rose from his bed and, springing with surprising agility, lunged towards him. Edison, mortified, pulled his eye away and clapped his hand over the hole in the wall.

"What is it?" the warden asked.

"He saw me," Edison hissed. "He saw me."

"No. He sees nothing. He sees a black hole only."

"His eye on the other side is pressed to this hole right now." Edison's palm remained flat over the opening.

"No, no. Try again. Look again."

After a moment Edison did so. But the prisoner was back on his cot, examining his fingers as before, then staring at the ceiling. What had happened? Had he simply imagined it?

Then came the loud clanking and turning of Kemmler's door locks. The amplification of sound in the prison corridors gave Edison an unaccustomed sensitivity.

"Someone is visiting."

"He sees a priest once a day."

Edison's eye surveyed the scene as the warden spoke close to his ear. "I'm allowing this now. Kemmler is making good progress. He will convert tomorrow. He appears to have taken God as his saviour. His jailers say he is repentant and determined to make his peace. Yes, he has undergone something of a personal conversion, if we are to believe it."

Neither the clergyman nor the murderer spoke, and it looked as through both were observing separate vows of silence until Kemmler knelt and the priest opened a leather breviary and read from it aloud. Edison couldn't hear the words, but imagined that these were probably the prisoner's last rites.

"I've seen enough. Take me back now." Edison was already feeling his way back along the starry corridor.

"Certainly."

"How do I get out? Show me out." He was desperate to go.

The warden had to dash after him. "But Mr Edison, I should show you to the chamber now—"

"Just show me to the gate."

"—where your chair is being readied. We must go the other way."

Edison stopped. "I have no wish to see it."

"But the men... we had presumed that... that you'd come in response to their request that you inspect the chair. The men know you are here and are waiting for you in the chamber."

* * *

A small round of applause met the famous man as he stepped into this other laboratory: the chamber of electrocution.

The warm reception was genuine, heartfelt. Four men in white dusters – Brown, with two younger men and one older – smiled as they made their admiration plain.

"Pay me no mind," Edison called as Brown stepped forward to shake his hand. "Please go on with your work as if I'm not here. I can't stay long."

But Brown was insistent. He introduced his two young assistants, then the older man, Dr Alfred Southwick. Edison judged this man to be over sixty. He had a Puritan's beard, a high moral manner suggesting self-assured maxims and unshatterable creeds.

"It is a dream come true, sir," the doctor said with the hint of a bow.

Brown continued: "It was actually Dr Southwick here who gave me the idea of electricity being used for this purpose in the first place."

"I see." Edison faced Southwick. "You're an electrician?"

"A dentist," Southwick replied with a smile. "But a progressive one."

Edison nodded, then looked past the man to the chair. "So, then... this is it?"

Brown stepped aside, creating an avenue to the death seat. "Yes sir. *That* is it." His face was gleaming with pride. "A summit of scientific achievement. And it will soon be the envy of every country."

Edison moved towards it. The heavy oak woodwork was even more solid than had been discussed and, rising from the seat back, was a short post topped with a triangular brace that projected a metal cup over the headrest. "Does it work?" Edison asked.

"Well, ha! Time will tell! Ha! Ha!"

"Does it work?" Edison repeated, deadly serious.

"All the tests would say so. We have been keenly aware that the whole world is watching the result of this experiment, and I am fully confident that Kemmler's death will be instantaneous."

Brown, Southwick and the assistants then edged forward, eager for the great man's praise – which, however, was slow to come. In fact,

Edison looked less and less pleased with the invention as the seconds passed. "So... the voltage you're aiming for?"

"Fifteen hundred volts, following your recommendation," Brown confirmed.

"And the... the AC generator. Where?"

"A thousand feet away. In the north-west wing."

Edison fiddled idly with the chair's leather arm straps. "And it is driven by—"

"A steam engine in the basement."

Edison bit his bottom lip, shaking his head slowly from side to side. "And the wires from this generator run—"

"Up onto the roof."

"The *roof*, you say?"

"And then directly down into this chamber."

"Directly?"

"Yes sir. Why? Is there—"

"And do you have any control over the current?"

Brown began to realize that Edison was unhappy, and he moved swiftly to placate him. "We have switches, meters and a regulator next door if you'd like to—"

"Why did you put them next door?"

"Well, well we thought that..." He shrugged. "I suppose because we decided it would look better to the public. Is something—"

"And how will you set the process going? What signal?"

"With that bell, sir. We will ring it twice." He pointed to a fireman's bell on the wall. "That is the signal. The dynamo will then be engaged, the current sent flowing, and the desired result achieved."

"I see." Edison's face darkened further.

Finally, Southwick could stand it no longer. "Is anything the matter, Mr Edison?"

169

"The matter? The *matter*, did you say?"

The dentist raised his voice. "The matter, yes. We trust that everything meets your approval, sir."

Edison scratched his chin, shifted his weight from leg to leg, smiled once, but generally looked ill at ease. He then said:

"No. I'm afraid… I'm afraid it doesn't meet my approval at all. The electrocution will have to be postponed. Warden, this chair is not ready."

A shock wave circulated the room. Brown's mouth fell open. "Mr Edison!"

Edison scratched his head, loosening the latest drizzle of dandruff. "Good you called me in. There is something wrong in the way you've set all this up. It'll take some time to get to the bottom of it. Understand?"

There was alarm on the face of Southwick. "Postponed?"

"Can't put my finger on it. When is the chair supposed to be ready? How many days?"

Brown was on the defensive: "Four. Uh… 7 a.m. August the sixth."

"Then I don't think the chair will be ready. Warden? You see? Just say – just say our understanding of how the chair will work is insufficient. Tell them that."

Warden Durston cast a nervous look at Brown, then back at Edison. "Sir? What do you mean?"

"I mean the execution will have to be postponed, possibly cancelled."

"Cancelled?"

"Mr Edison," Brown said, "I assure you—"

Edison's voice reached its full strength: "I said, it won't be ready!"

The angry force of this froze the gathering, as Edison began to pace about the room, sometimes circling the chair, sometimes the men. "The Legislature will just have to be told, Brown" – he batted dismissively the wires spiralling down from the ceiling – "that further improvements and testing are vital."

"But *none* are necessary," Brown contradicted bravely.

"And what do you know?" Edison rounded on Brown, advancing quickly until they were but two feet apart.

"We—" Brown inclined backwards.

"Are you even an electrician? I am the world's foremost electrical inventor, and if I say it's not ready, it's not ready."

Southwick directed his voice, if only a whisper, at Brown. "Tell him about the test. Tell him."

Brown obeyed. "But... we have just ten minutes ago finished a successful test of the equipment. And it was a complete success."

"How? You put to death another prisoner just before I got here? What – what did you test?"

"Dr Southwick."

"Southwick?"

"The Doctor sat in the chair. We ran the system at between ten and twenty volts."

"Ten and twenty? That proves – what? Nothing! And if you think it does, then let me perform a test with the Doctor in the chair."

"Of course, if you wish," Brown retorted, without first consulting the doctor: he was desperate to save the chair. "Doctor?" Southwick looked extremely alarmed. "Doctor? Would you kindly oblige again?" Brown motioned towards the chair. "Mr Edison would like to repeat the test."

"Please," Edison added.

"Would you mind removing your jacket so we can run another test?"

"Another test?" the Doctor wanly replied. "I thought—"

"Please. For Mr Edison's sake."

The Doctor didn't immediately respond, but under the weight of the party's stares his hands eventually rose from his sides and none too surely drew from his shoulders his thigh-length jacket. "How much – voltage – this time?"

Edison had a firm idea. "Between 100 and 200. Which should be fine, if Mr Brown is correct and 'no more tests are necessary'."

Brown went to the door and called to an assistant manning the dynamo. "Mr Jackson! One hundred volts!"

Edison corrected him. "Two hundred would be better."

"Two hundred!" echoed Brown, who then went over to the Doctor and fastened him in place, quickly securing his arms, drawing one strap around his chest and another around his legs. Finally, the metal cap was pressed down on the dentist's head for the second time that morning.

Southwick tried to keep up a bold face, but he was clearly agitated.

"Thank you doctor," Edison said. "And let's just hope there is no slippage."

"Slippage?"

"Of the dynamo's drive belt." He then said to Brown: "Remember that Golden Lab—"

"—rador, yes." Brown nodded.

"That you burned to a cinder? Let's hope we have none of that kind of accident."

Dr Southwick's eyes widened in fright, but before he could speak Brown drew the leather mask over his face, whereupon only muffled words could be heard coming from him. As Edison joined the effort to tighten all the straps, he said: "Remember? The current fell right away to nothing – and then the belt engaged again" – jerking tight a strap – "and sent 400 volts down the line." Southwick was becoming frantically agitated: his lips flexed and, as he struggled against the tightness of the bonds, his muffled words rose louder. "Did you feel nauseous, Brown?" Edison asked. "The poor dog. Not that we need fear 400 volts this time – given Mr Brown assurance that 'no more tests are necessary'."

As Edison moved over to the signal bell, Brown tried to soothe the terrorized doctor. "It's fine, Alfred. We'll take all precautions."

Gripping the bell rope Edison called: "Are we ready? Shall we begin? Is your man standing by at the dynamo?"

Brown said, "He is." Then, bending again to the flinching Southwick, he added: "Are you ready, Alfred? Don't worry."

"And another at the controls?" shouted Edison.

"Umm," said Brown, worried about Southwick's lack of composure.

"Is there someone at the controls?!"

"There... is... yes," Brown managed. Again he said to his friend, "It's OK. It will be fine."

But by now the dentist was struggling hard under his restraints and clearly wished to be released.

"Then let's run some power into this chair of yours," Edison announced, "which has been tested beyond any doubt."

Southwick could no longer be soothed. Brown raised his hand. "Mr Edison, the Doctor seems to be in some distress."

Ignoring this, Edison said: "The signal is two rings, is it not?"

"Mr Edison... the Doctor..."

But it was too late. Edison rang the bell once. "What's that you say?"

"Wait!" called Brown.

Edison prepared to tug the bell rope again. "I can't hear you."

"STOP!!!"

But before anyone could act, Edison jerked again on the bell rope. "Two!" The subterranean rumble of the generator began, and all except Edison heard the whirr of the dynamo 1,000 feet away in the north-west wing. It was too late to stop the current now.

"No! Wait!" Brown leapt towards his friend. With two hands and with fearless urgency Brown went to unfasten the mask that muffled but could not silence the Doctor's cries of "Let me out! Let me out!"

"Two more peals!" Brown called to Edison, fearful of receiving a shock himself. "The signal to stop! The signal to stop! Two more peals!"

"The signal to *what*?" Edison put his hand to his ear, his other hand motionless on the bell rope.

At last the mask was off and the doctor was able to be fully heard once again as he cried, "Turn it off! Turn it off!" and Brown rushed to the alarm bell and rang it twice himself, then twice again, calling loudly, as the sound of the dynamo began to fall away. "It's OK, Alfred! It's off! It's off! It's off. It's OK. It's off."

But Southwick would not be easily calmed. "It's not off. It's *not* off! Slippage! Slippage! Slippage!"

Brown returned to his colleague. "It's off! Calm down, Alfred. Alfred!" Finally, he slapped the Doctor's face.

A sudden silence followed one last cry of "Slippage…"

"It's over. You're unharmed," Brown concluded.

Edison crossed back to the chair and started on the straps. "Let me help."

Brown resisted. "It's fine."

"I want to help."

"Good Lord," Southwick stammered, as freedom began to return to one limb after another. "Good Lord. Most upsetting. Most upsetting. I never volunteered for the real thing. I was not prepared—"

With Edison's assistance, Brown raised Southwick from the chair.

"My fault, Doctor," Edison offered. "It's quite clear you are the wrong person to submit to this trial."

Brown glanced fearfully at the inventor. "The wrong person?"

Edison sat in the chair himself. "It should be me. Strap me in. Let's go again."

Brown, gripping the doctor by the arm, could only stare.

"I said: strap me in."

"Sir, what is it you want?"

"I've told you. Admit the system is flawed – or else ring the bell. If you are ready to experiment on a criminal, then start with me. First me, then you."

"I have done nothing wrong. What are you saying?"

"That we're behaving like the criminals we judge."

"Criminals?"

"You're a fool! A horse's ass! I made use of you. And I blame myself. So here I am, on my rightful throne. Now ring the bell!"

"Please, Mr Edison," Brown protested, "get out of the Westing-house chair!"

"I've got a new name for this chair: the Wall Street chair. This chair is meant for us, Harold, have no doubt, for you and for me – fool servants of a master whose only aim is to remove the last barriers holding greed at bay. The bell!"

Brown's nerves could take it no more. "Very well. I will ask for a postponement. I'll write to the Legislature today."

"And say what?"

"Say… that… more testing is necessary. We've… discovered f—"

"Faults."

"—faults… in the method. Profound faults."

Satisfied, Edison finally rose from the chair. "And explain that the complete failure of the system was unforeseeable. It may never be viable." Dusting off his hands, Edison confronted his collaborator one last time and looked emotionally into the man's eyes. "Do I have your word?"

"You have it."

"I can't hear you."

"You have it."

"And is it still worth having?"

"I trust that it is."

Edison extended a hand and Brown shook it. "We are citizens of eternity, Mr Brown. Remember that." And with this the inventor left the room, immediately followed by the warden.

The silence that followed was broken by Brown. "Forget him."

Southwick turned to look at Brown. "What do you mean?"

"Forget him. He's losing his mind. He's yesterday's man. There's nothing wrong with the chair. Let's get to work. We only have four days."

As Brown went back to work, the Doctor remained confused. "Forget him?"

"The world is changing fast, Alfred. And I am sad to say it of one once so mighty, but that man is not taking his irrelevance well."

* * *

On the morning of the execution, Morgan found his way to the offices of George Westinghouse. He was immediately shown in.

The two large, imposing men regarded each other as two nations might do, across a vast gulf of culture, philosophy and personal interest.

"What is it you want?"

"George. How the devil are you?"

"You tell me. What do you want, Morgan?"

"Let's say... we are two serious men... who need to have a conversation... about the inevitable."

"Before you say anything, I want you to know, I won't be intimidated. You can't frighten me the way you frighten others."

"I have no desire to intimidate or frighten."

"I know how you work. Anyone who resists you, you coerce. Morganization? I know the catchphrase. 'The futility of battle', right? 'Combine... for the good of the common man'. Well, I work along different lines than you bankers. I believe in letting the best man win. Sometimes the law of the jungle is just fairer."

"But I already know who the best man is."

"Oh, I'm sure you do."

"You are. You and Tesla."

Westinghouse angled his head and looked at Morgan through his left – and best – eye. "What is the name of this game?"

"George – let's be straight. This electricide... it's a sideshow. A low farce. History remembers the hard numbers. Your current, AC, is cheaper. You won on the day your price went below ours. That's all that will count in the end."

"Then why? Why the dirty fight? Why go ahead with this – this grotesque spectacle? Is it really worth the cost just to sully my name? The Westinghouse Chair? How dare you! To name a death chair after me, you and your wizard sidekick, and then have the gall to come to my office?"

"Cigar?"

"No. I suspect it will explode. 'Alternating is the killer current.' Why say it? Why go to all that trouble to discredit me, if you knew I was going to win in the end?"

Morgan moved to the window. Outside it New York, a feast for the restless eye of any adventurer. "Look out there, look out the window, a new city. One made in stone. Houses that will outlast the seasonal cold and the lousy maintenance. Posterity, George. We are a flicker of light, you and I, a brief illumination between two infinities of darkness. In the end it's the future we serve. And of the two of us, I'm the better servant. But you

ANTHONY McCARTEN

have something I need. I couldn't go around you, so I must join with you."

"My God! Good Heavens almighty! I thought *I* played rough. You know who I suddenly feel very sorry for? Thomas Alva Edison. And I never thought I'd say that. I admired him – did you know that? He was a hero of mine. He proved to all of us who wanted to change things that anything can be changed. With two hands, a clear head, a good breakfast – you can change almost anything. But he didn't see *you* coming."

Morgan turned back to Westinghouse. One prodigious moustache faced another. "We're inevitable, George. You and I. The bankers are moving in, turning the great fiefdoms into public companies, floating them on the stock exchange, keeping only the famous surnames intact for their letterheads. Men of high principles, defenders of the poor, fully independent, unrestricted, who, upon their deaths will be honoured in every civic square and department store. Marble and bronze will succeed our flesh. But such a transformation of public finance must be managed with enormous care, because what we build today will drive all the centuries ahead... and the future, when looking back for its birthplace, will stop at these times, remember these offices, the names written on these doors, and say, 'Yes, this was how it all began.'"

Westinghouse, almost in appreciation, shook his head. "Pierpont – you are so dishonest that even the opposite of what you say isn't true. You won't pull such a mountain of fleece over my eyes."

"Good. Keep your eyes well shorn, George. And read this." He produced a document from his vest pocket. "A new company. A combination. Based on your AC system. Capitalized at twelve million dollars. Run by *professional* men. Under the terms of the merger, Edison General Electric agrees to a slightly inferior stock position, but I'd like to retain the name, at least in part."

"In part?"

Morgan flicked open his jacket to reveal a waistcoat devoid of buttons and only half-fastened by a curious contraption. "General Electric. Simpler." And with a noisy flourish he tugged upwards on a device which fully drew together the two sheets of fabric – *zip*!

Westinghouse took the document and looked over the first paragraph. "Has Edison... has he approved all this?"

"Not yet. I'm anticipating his resignation."

Westinghouse roared with laughter at this, looked up and shook his head once more, his last suspicions giving way to fatalistic admiration. "Good Lord. Is nothing sacred any more? Is nothing to be sacred ever again?" Finally he proffered his hand, and with a smile – one lit by sunlight reflected in through the windows off buildings built from the public hope of more money for everyone – Morgan shook it.

* * *

Young men were already perched in the maples in front of the prison, and from every lamp-post and vantage point hundreds directed their eyes above the perimeter wall to the high, vine-wrapped window which rumour alone had established was Kemmler's cell.

A dense crowd had also formed on the platform opposite the railway station across the road. People on their way to work swelled their numbers until it was impossible for pedestrians or traffic to pass in the street. Finally, a bell rang. Self-appointed lookouts in the trees decided that this could only mean that the murderer had been killed and so waved their handkerchiefs. A public cheer went up. The wait was over.

"He's dead! He's dead! He's dead!" came the united chant. Excited men grabbed and kissed their wives. Others threw hats. Children finger-whistled and strangers embraced like old acquaintants. Edison's name was pronounced with admiration and Westinghouse's with ridicule. Phrase-makers with ready lines loudly dubbed it "a triumph of civilization".

But the excitement soon died down as contradictory details spread that the bell, located in the prison kitchen, had been nothing more than a notice to the gatekeepers to open the doors for the new intake of kitchen staff, most of whom were in the crowd outside. Struggling to cope with the anticlimactic notion that their great celebration had been for a worker's shift change, the throng initially refused to step aside, unable to see why they should give up their advantage and compromise their view of the gates for a mere half-dozen cooks.

In the end, however, the dispute was resolved, and when the kitchen workers had been admitted, the long wait resumed.

* * *

The night had been a long one, and back at West Orange his writing hand was numb with deletions. The Dresden clock on the wall was not far off 6 a.m. – and by eight, allowing one hour for Morgan's man in the death chamber to cross the street to the freight station and send a wire confirming that the event had happened without a hitch – he hoped to sleep soundly for all the days that were left to him on earth.

He put down his pen and shook feeling back into his hand. He had just completed a long letter, among the most important of his life, and the crucial paragraph read:

As you all may have observed, I am pretty well broken down right now with overwork, and I am going to go away for a while. I think up until now I have performed every duty asked of me, made every concession, and I would now ask you not to oppose my gradual retirement from the lighting business, which will enable me to enter fresh and more congenial fields of work.

He put down the pages, sighed and signed.

With this letter, to be sent to Pierpont Morgan, he drew a curtain on twenty-six years of work – work that had brought him world fame, but which had also drawn him into affairs intolerable to his disposition, doing irreparable damage. He folded the letter and slipped it into a manila envelope.

"Sir?" the maid said at his shoulder, leaning into his left ear. "Will you take a liddle soup?"

He shook his head. She left him alone.

* * *

Kemmler was shown into the chamber. He had been given a monk's tonsure. The shaven patch on his crown was a vivid disc of white. He was immaculately turned out. In a new suit, lacking only a flower in the buttonhole to make him the nervous groom awaiting his bride, he looked beyond the chair to the twenty nervous faces of the watchful invitees. He had shown the graces of a saint for three months now, and nothing that life could throw at him this day would change his manner. As his name was announced, he bowed and surprised everyone by speaking.

"Gentlemen, I see no ladies, I wish you all good luck." The guests were taken aback. They could well have done without this display of his humanity. He had more: "I believe I am going to a good place, and I am ready to die by electricity. I'm glad I am not going to be hanged. It will not give me any pain. I'm not afraid. My faith is too firm to be shaken. I have never been so happy in my life as I have been here, in this prison—"

The warden intervened. "That's enough, Bill."

He bowed again. He adjusted the lapels of his suit, a gift from the jailers, and went to sit on a small kitchen stool set beside the death chair, as rehearsed. Seeing this, the warden stepped forward and Kemmler, noticing the warden's action, saw that the time had come, and so sat down in the death chair itself.

"Now take your time," he said, almost jokingly. He was nervous, but he faintly smiled. "And do it right, warden. There is no rush. I don't want to take any chances on this thing, you know."

"I will, Bill," the warden stammered. "I'll do that."

He now needed to ask Kemmler to rise again, so that he could check that his carefully pressed suit had been cut away at the spine as to allow a clean contact with the electrode. He found that the suit had been adapted as planned, but that the shirt beneath had not. The warden asked for a pocket knife, quickly bent and cut the hole himself.

"Everything all right?" Kemmler asked.

"You can sit down now, Bill."

"As you say, Mr Durston."

Kemmler sat again, and the time had come for the straps and helmet to be fastened. He shook his head to test the cap's tightness. Finding it slightly too loose for his liking, and having been schooled in the rudiments of the procedure, he asked: "Push it down tight, warden. Don't you worry about me. As tight as you like."

The warden's hands were now visibly shaking as he pulled the chinstrap tighter. "God bless you, Kemmler."

"I wanna do the best I can."

"You have, Bill. You have. I'll make sure it won't hurt you."

Before the mask was drawn over his face, Kemmler took the chance to speak one last time. "Well, I wish everybody good luck. I've done the best I can. And I can't do any better than that." His face showed that there was much more to say, but it was then muzzled with leather. When the warden asked another question, the prisoner could only utter a muffled sound that was inaudible to the audience. Warden Durston backed away. "All right," he said, throwing a pale look at his assistants.

Then he loudly spoke the words which were the secret signal for the electrocution to begin: "Goodbye William Kemmler!" – and walked to the door.

The designated moment had come.

The bell on the wall was rung twice. The sound of the Westinghouse generator rose.

THOMAS

The current passed into it. It glowed brilliantly, but it did not last. Surrounded by his men, he searched for a new filament, placed ever more far-fetched materials between the points of a lamp's armatures and let the current pass into each: celluloid, cedar, cotton soaked in tar, cork, the skim of a rice pudding, architect's drawing paper, a hair from Batchelor's beard, a thread of spider's web: this last gave off a green but beautiful phosphorescence. But in the end they all failed… Pfff! Pfff! Pfff!… the filaments falling as a drizzle of black powder.

And then, on the third and final day, Batchelor, at his table opposite Edison's, fashioned a loop of charred cardboard. The air was slowly drawn from a glass bulb. The "horseshoe" was set inside it and a current passed into it…

* * *

This time the old man failed to be shaken from his thoughts by the boy's questions.

"Sir? Sir? Are you alright? Shall I get a doctor?"

Distressed to see that the snow-white head had sunken onto the chest, that the eyes were closed and that the only sign of life was a very shallow breath, the boy forgot himself and betrayed the secret he had been protecting this last hour.

"Mr Edison? Mr Edison? Are you all right?"

Realizing his slip-up at once, but also that nothing was lost, because the inventor was unconscious, he rose and shouted: "You just hold on, all right? I'm going to get a doctor. Can you hear me? I'm going to get a doctor for you." Taking his suitcase with him, he turned and ran away down the platform.

The old man seemed to revive, if only partially. His memory was roaming freely again...

* * *

Charley. He cried out in pain. Weakened by a night of tormented hallucinations, Edison's young nephew, Charley, in a Paris loft (on the night table leeches lay bloated in jars), screamed at his lover for putting his body "between the poles of a battery". Mystified by such outbursts, the lover fumbled with a syringe, injected more morphine, and then administered a purgative of castor oil. Draining the cup was Charley's last act.

And what did the young, lost American traveller think he was drinking in that final moment? Champagne on the Rue de Bach? Federweißer aboard a ferry on the Rhine? The draught took effect at once. Charley vomited and evacuated his bowels for ninety minutes, a last torture, until...

* * *

...The cardboard horseshoe lamp glowed all night. The lamp was born.

Two days later Edison would speak with a journalist:

"We sat and looked at the filament, nearly thirty of us in all, and it continued to burn. And the longer it burned, the more fascinated we were. None of us could go to bed, and there was no sleep for any of us for another forty hours. We just sat there and watched. And the lamp just burned on and on and on."

EDISON

The *New York Times* reported it. The *New York Post* and the *Buffalo Express* also carried the story.

"And then the power was cut. And his death proclaimed. The body relaxed, but the fingers of Kemmler's right hand had closed up so tightly during the event that this observer noted that the exceptionally well-groomed nails had actually penetrated the flesh – and blood dripped off the arm of the chair. A most gruesome sight indeed."

In his matted clothes, locked inside his study and nursing a nascent hermit's beard as he read, the world's most famous inventor suffered an attack of moral vertigo so severe he twice had to fight back nausea.

He had strained science, as well as his own reputation. As Robespierre had mangled the ideas of Rousseau, so he had betrayed Faraday. His mind recoiled from the dripping sound of the nail-punctured hand, each red drop striking the floor in a series of mental detonations. But there was no escaping it, and he picked up the newspaper again. "The warden examined the body and then pronounced the ordeal over. What physicians know as death spots had appeared on the skin. Kemmler's body was still. Seventeen seconds had passed. It was just 6.43 a.m. It had taken only seventeen seconds. A second doctor, nodding his head, confirmed: 'Yes. He is dead. The man is dead.' With this, the assembled witnesses, who had sat still and silent up to this point, gave breath to a sigh. The great strain was over."

ANTHONY McCARTEN

At his desk, Edison put down one paper and took up another, racing to the same point in the narrative. "The doctors then converged on the dead man and poked at his skin. Dr Southwick turned to address the audience in a state of great excitement. 'There,' he said with visible relief, 'there is the culmination of ten years of work and study. We live in a higher civilization from this day.' A second doctor added, 'Undo him. The body can be taken away.' It had been the most testing afternoon that everybody in that chamber had ever been asked to endure."

Edison rubbed his eyes. Was he crying? The effort of reading this was immense. The telegram he had received the previous night from his informant within the death chamber had denied him any of these details. In fact, the cable had misled him entirely, overemphasizing the success of the event. His head now reeled with dark thoughts. Where was Morgan now? On his boat with an heiress bound for Egypt? At anchor with his courtesans and his purloined works of art? Would this event slow the banker's march, or still for one second the beat of his executive drum? Or was his advance now inexorable and invincible already? He picked up a third newspaper.

"The first man in the gallery to rise to his feet shook his head and looked relieved to have survived the event himself. But as the warden began to unfasten the chair's straps, Dr Spitzka pointed out that the wound on the prisoner's hand continued to ooze blood. Silence descended on the chamber. Was the doctor correct? Such a phenomenon would require, surely, a beating heart. All eyes focused on the slow but continuous dripping of blood from the arm of the chair and the hand upon it, which was pierced at the palm with its own nails. Those witnesses hoping to leave right away found the doors closed to them again while a few in the front rows leant closer. Two minutes had gone by since the current had been cut, but there was still clear evidence of movement in Kemmler's body. Finally the sound of the man's first attempt to breathe again became audible. The honoured gentlemen in the gallery rose from their chairs impulsively. One shouted: 'Great God! He is alive! He is alive!' Another: 'Turn on the current.' A third: 'See, he breathes!' An assistant, receiving a nod from the ghostly-white Dr Southwick, bolted from the chamber.

"'For God's sake, kill him and have it over!' cried a member of the press – but then, unable to bear the strain, the same man fell on the floor in a dead faint. District Attorney Quimby groaned and rushed from the room to vomit."

Edison jerked loose his collar and went to the window, throwing it open. He could hardly breathe deeply enough. Dear God! He gripped the frame and wavered, dizzy, nauseous, his own stomach in knots.

"Forty-five minutes in all. Forty-five minutes – that is how long it took to kill the murderer Kemmler. At its climax a blue flame shot out of his metal skull cap. Wisps of smoke rose from behind his back. Boiling urine ran across the floor. The base of his spine caught fire and set his clothes alight. They had roasted him, filling the room with the smell of over-cooked beef. Afterwards his body was so hot it could not be touched for a further ninety minutes."

Edison had suppressed his private doubts about the chair's failings until too late. And, worse than that, he'd closed his mind to many alternatives. How had this happened? By what corrosive process? He returned to his desk. He forced himself to read the verdicts of the world upon his actions.

"A sacrifice to the designs of Wall Street's money men," the *Times* began, "was offered today in the person of William Kemmler, the Buffalo murderer. He died this morning under the most revolting circumstances, and with his death there was placed to the discredit of these profit-mongers an execution that was a disgrace to civilization..." The *Chronicle* of London: "It was a scene worthy of the darkest chambers of the Inquisition in the sixteenth century..."

A sage-like columnist for the London *Standard* even took pity on Kemmler. A murderer, yes. But what hope for the civilized if we sank to the methods of the evildoer? "I would rather see ten hangings than one electricide. This would surely be the last execution of this kind." The writer then concluded: "Alternating current is clearly not the killer current that Mr Thomas Edison and company had made it out to be. On the contrary, the hideous experiment has vindicated it, showing it to be so congenial that the combined genius of the electrical industry could not easily snuff out a man with it."

Harold Brown, in complete denial, said: "The prisoner was killed instantly and painlessly within the first second." The *New York Post*, on a more philosophical note, spoke the uncreated thoughts of many: "Heretofore the proudest claim of science has been to save, or at least prolong human life. In this instance it has been disastrously diverted from its course."

These printed words rushed through the inventor at his desk until he slumped back in his chair. His own heart had virtually stopped.

* * *

In the club rooms of the New York Yacht Club, Pierpont Morgan put down the last of the morning's newspapers, ordered a glass of brandy to help him digest three analgesics, then tore open the envelope which had been placed on the tray table beside the game of chess he had begun earlier. "Dear Morgan, as you all may have observed, I am pretty well broken down right now..." Morgan quickly scanned the rest of the letter, then put it down. He lit a large Havana, became thoughtful for a moment and then returned to studying the chess game in which he was one pawn up.

His opponent had gone to the water closet, and the chance to study the game in private, and at length, was a mercy given his relative inexperience. Chess was a beautiful, if cold game. Naturally Morgan wanted to win at it, but he wasn't ready to put in the time necessary to become an expert. When he wasn't working, which was almost never, he yearned for human distractions, intimate contact, animate pleasures – and this need would not be answered by pushing wooden figurines about a chequered field.

He continued to work too hard – this he knew full well. For all his success, it had been years since his life had truly been his own, his to live freely. His wealth had bought him satisfaction, but his life… his life gave him headaches, fits of black depression, little peace. The bright, youthful pursuit of power was replaced by the dull preservation of it, and it was small recompense. He had little choice, now, but to increase his ambitions on a daily basis, extending his influence farther and farther afield – to do anything less was viewed by the world, and by him, as ingratitude. And for all his faults, he was not ungrateful.

He was rejoined at last by his guest.

"Forgif me, Mr Morgan."

"Pierpont, please. Your move."

The guest was breathing hard, had clearly darted outside just now. "The evening editions are out. I stop to read. Edison and that chair. All over the front page. All over!"

"Yes. A disaster for him. Your move."

"Serves him right, I says. On the wall has been the writing for a long time."

Nikola Tesla barely deliberated before moving his king's bishop into an unexpected position, threatening two of Morgan's pieces at once. "You fell into my trap," crowed the Serb.

"Holy God!" muttered Morgan as he comprehended the damage that would soon be done. "You're a genius. This is just further proof. Look at that. This is terrible. I should resign at once. My queen is—"

"Yes," Tesla said, "doomed."

"If I move it—"

"You cannot. You would be placing yourself in check."

"You have me."

"Yes."

"Devastating."

"Yes. Devastating."

Morgan sighed. "Good Lord. I resign. I resign."

"And Tesla accepts your resignation."

Morgan shook his head. "Ha! And you know the funny thing? I thought I was winning. I was just sitting here while you were gone thinking, I'm winning, I'm winning."

"An illusion," Tesla said.

Morgan shook his head again. "Evidently. Now let me finish telling you my proposal. Then I must dash. I have two more meetings before dinner. One with Mr Westinghouse. A fine chap. A man of real principle."

"Yes, go on. I like this talk. Of a marriage majestical. This world of yours and mine, run by a financial—"

"Elite. Precisely. But hear me out. Order a drink, Nikola, and hear me out. The world will never make so much sense again."

* * *

The mood at the inaugural meeting of the Edison General Electric company was brittle.

Edison had taken to dressing like a tramp again. No one had been able to reach him for weeks. This meeting, a truly historic one, should have taken place two months before, but Edison had proved impossible to pin down. For a time, right after the Kemmler episode, he had gone missing. Not even Charles Batchelor had known where his employer was hiding. One rumour had it that he was ill, close to death – that he had fled to Key Largo. But in the end reports filtered back that he'd simply given everyone the slip and gone into the hills of New Jersey, to begin a search for a supposed source of iron ore and deposits of *aurum purum* – gold.

The board of EGE was now fully aware of Edison's decision – relayed by letter – to leave behind the electrical industry for good. And although impossible to accept at the time, the passing of days had made it easier and easier to imagine a world without him.

Today the board members were arrayed against him in spectacular solidarity, men now wary of having their fortunes in the hands of a – what was he now? – a prospector? Furthermore, Edison's long and public opposition to alternating current had left him isolated, especially since it had become clear that AC was the safer form of electrical delivery. J.P. Morgan, at the head of the anti-Edison faction – orchestrating, goading, dominating, combining – had merely to point out that no company could afford to harbour in their ranks someone who had no use for the sole commodity in which the company traded.

Edison was asked to sit anywhere he liked. He chose the middle of the table, where his chances of hearing what was said would be greatest. With the exception of Pierpont Morgan and Nikola Tesla, all the other men were strangers. In fact, he felt himself surrounded not just by strangers, but by an entirely new breed of men – company managers – and he could tell by their deference that they expected anger from him. But he mocked this with a look of disinterest. He was agitated, eager only to have this done with, desperate only to return to the hills.

He glanced at Morgan. The nose, the famous nose, was having one of its cyclical periods of eruption, and was today a cross-hatching of reds, whites and purples. The banker's sharp blue eyes, however, were as quick as they had ever been. The two men had not met in months, and they had only fed on rumours of the other. Brief glances between them now were the only attempts to cast doubt on the most outrageous of these rumours. To Morgan, Edison did not look crazy – not today. And to Edison, he could see no evidence that Morgan was imperilled by syphilis.

And what reasons remained for them to meet anyway? Neither man had a talent for intimacy. Their mutual admiration had faded. And as to Morgan's vision of a union between them, everyone knew that the banker and Billy Vanderbilt had just funded Westinghouse's ambition to harness Niagara Falls in order to generate enough alternating current to supply the entire state. Appointed to oversee all this? Nikola Tesla.

Charles Coffin, the dapper new president of Edison General Electric, began with a booming voice, no doubt for Edison's sake. "Gentlemen, if we can come to order, it falls on me to announce, and with no small degree of pleasure, that a giant combination of our company with that of our main AC competitors, unprecedented in size and implication, has been proposed and latterly agreed, barring the signature of our founder Mr Edison, here present." Coffin took a breath, his hands clasped behind his back. "The aim, of course, is to form a single and unique… I believe the new word is *conglomeration*." He glanced at Morgan, who nodded. "Its reach and influence will not only extend from shore to shore, but at the same time will bridge the great plains of continental Europe.

"And so it is this board's opinion that we should not resist such a merger. The times compel it, society compels it, the simple needs of the people compel it. By reducing our costs in every area, by pooling our expertise to create the best products, and *before* anyone else can, we can be certain of profits… certain of them… in a way that no other company, or perhaps very few, have ever enjoyed in a free nation.

"Accordingly, monumental work has been done by both our companies... and of course by Mr Morgan. But we do not forget for one second the contribution of Mr Edison here present, or the impact... the great impact of his bulb, without which none of us would be here today." There was a small, almost patronizing round of applause. "He is truly... truly the joint architect of what we are about to summon... summon into being today. The true inventor of the future."

Edison's eyes sought Morgan's. The banker, perhaps sensing them, kept looking at the speaker, perhaps so that shame would not register on that rugged Welsh face. Edison lowered his stare to the table – he noted that the banker's gloves sported, at the wrist, a zipper in place of a stud. What an operator! The all-new clasp locker on the wrist of Pierpont Morgan – it meant only one thing: that the future of that contraption was assured. It would survive, prosper, dominate for certain. Henceforth, God help the makers of buttons!

"Mr Edison?" Coffin said over light applause. " Do you wish to speak? Mr Edison? MR EDISON? DO YOU WISH TO SPEAK?"

The inventor looked up, faced Coffin with an air of weary resignation. "Finish this up and then let me go. How many shares do I still have in this company?"

Coffin replied instantly: "If you include your wife's holdings as well, then... about... five or six percent."

"Is that all?"

"I believe so."

Edison nodded. Whenever money had been tight, he had sold his own shares. And now the company, which over the years he had so often saved, was his to save no longer. "Then you need hardly give me the time of day. Proceed."

Coffin nodded and, after a respectful pause, resumed. "And so it is a mighty day, gentlemen. A day that will go down in the annals of modern business. For under the terms of the merger as agreed this

195

last week, EGE agrees to a slightly inferior stock position in the new combined company, but in an act of symbolic importance… our new partners are happy for their names not to appear in the title of the new entity. And so I am delighted to announce that the new name for our company shall be…"

And with this he walked to the far wall and tugged back a cloth draped over a plaque. The new company insignia was revealed. The two-word name was read in silence by all.

Edison rose. "If you'll excuse me, I have business now in New Jersey."

* * *

Three years.

One thousand and ninety-five days.

Twenty-six thousand, two hundred and eighty hours.

One million, five hundred seventy-six thousand, eight hundred minutes.

Mina plucked out a recent letter and pressed it into Batch's hand. "It's from Thomas."

Loamy fingerprints had dirtied the envelope.

"Ever since he ran off into the hills after that horrible business with the chair three years ago, ever since he ran away from us all, he has written a letter every two days. Don't ask me what he's doing up there in those hills. His letters say nothing. Explain nothing. You know him. What happened to him?"

Batchelor shrugged. Just off the train, newly returned from England, where he had lived for the last three years, he had responded to Mina's desperate cry of help, but about the inner change that had come over his old friend all he knew was practical facts: that Edison made good on his threat to turn his back on electrical invention for good, and in so doing had left his family to mine the New Jersey hills, to dig unprofitable holes, in search of God only knew what.

"In letter after letter," she said, "he keeps saying he will change himself and make up for his faults. His faults are obvious enough, but he seems to mean something else."

Batchelor could only shrug. "Englishness" once more ruled his manners, and it was impolite to venture theories on matrimonial affairs.

"Is he really looking for gold up in those hills?" she asked.

"I... I think there may be a little iron ore up there, but no gold."

"Perhaps he is trying to turn the former into the latter?"

Batchelor smiled. What a lovely woman! "Perhaps so. I should not put it past him. From the outset there was always something of the alchemist in him."

The next morning, at her insistence, Batch agreed to read several of Edison's letters. In the parlour, while tea was being served to him, he turned the dirty pages. From them he could draw no conclusion, nor offer Mina any analysis about the friend of his youth. But he did agree to venture into the hills of New Jersey in an attempt to draw the famous hermit back into civilized society after the inexplicable exile of three years.

Mina called for a coach in front of the house. He collected his hat. Outside on the street he shook her hand fondly.

"Just bring him back," she begged, "if you can."

Batchelor climbed on board and tapped the arm of the driver.

* * *

The small wayside station at Ogdensburg was empty when the Englishman arrived. The water trough was as dried up as the potted plants abandoned on the station's window sills. Even the occasional shoe and discarded hat lay about, and the doors of the depot lay wide open, the luggage trolley tipped on its side – evidence everywhere of a hasty evacuation.

Taking his bearings, he walked north up the road into the hills. It had been three years since he'd been here last, at the start of this bizarre venture to mine these hills for whatever they contained. Back then, the hills were being rocked every fifteen minutes with a new explosion. A steam shovel mindlessly dug a hole so deep for itself that it was never able to be returned back to ground level. Twenty-four hours a day the Edison men had burrowed into the earth, blasting, smashing, conveying ore and useless rubble back to the surface. Vast sums were being spent every hour, the entire payout from the Morgan takeover of Edison General Electric being wasted. One year had become two. The hills were ground down, the rocks carried away in railway cars. Edison had made a handful of visits to see his family, but always returned unhappy, ordering a fresh offensive on the earth. Finally, the money dried up and, one day in August, when Edison could no longer pay the three hundred men in his employ, those white ghosts coated in alabaster walked off the job, never to return.

Edison's decision to stay on almost alone at Ogden was the most peculiar of all. He sought no luxuries, denied himself every pleasure. However, his letter-writing to his wife reached a climax.

In his correspondence he intended to explain his predicament, but he had to conceal so much from her, for fear of alarming her, that in the end these letters were no more than bland enquiries into her health and that of the children. His real feelings were so encrypted in banal chit-chat that it would have required a mind-reader to decipher the desperate messages beneath.

Batch made slow progress up the incline. Now in his fiftieth year, his health was deteriorating and he had a constant pain on the left side. Recently he had tried a self-cure: he had sat in a large wooden box he'd built in his garage and bombarded himself with X-rays three hours a day while enjoying the readings given by his daughter of the later and less celebrated works of Shakespeare, plays which Batch suspected weren't written by the bard at all, but by some forgotten, unsung assistant.

The X-ray treatments had not worked. In the last three years he had hung up his white duster for good, returning to London to immerse himself in family life, to enjoy small pleasures – how to whistle with vibrato, to sleep in a chair in the garden at 11 a.m. waking just in time for lunch, to play solitaire after supper – all the while making notes for new inventions, but only so as to rejoice in *not* pursuing them. He woke now in a state that was the opposite of anxiety, and greeted his increasing insignificance as if it were a beautiful sunrise.

He reached the mine. What buildings! What scale! The concept was absurd. What had Alva been thinking? The rollers in the rock-crusher were almost ten storeys high. The building housing them as big as a department store. Without question this place was the work of a mind utterly unafraid of failure – perhaps one actively courting it.

Finally he saw a lone figure. Batch quickened his pace: "Sir! I'm looking for Mr Edison. Mr Edison?"

The man was a foreigner: a pipe-smoking French-Canadian, hard to understand until he stopped and pointed his pipe: "Ze Monsieur over zere! You find him over zere."

"There? Where is there?"

"Zere. He is in ze Monastery."

"The Monastery?"

The term was ironic. The place was in fact a broken-backed wooden shack hidden behind a grove of cottonwoods. As Batchelor came round the side of the hut, he caught his first sighting in three years of his old friend and collaborator. How he'd changed! Edison looked

199

to be napping in a rocker on the porch, the now snow-white head resting on his chest in the sunlight.

Batchelor stopped, observing the trademark white duster soiled and grey, its tails flapping in the breeze. Judging from his look, Alva had been mining up here with his bare hands. When he crept closer, Batch noted that his feet were pushing the rocker in gentle motion – the great man was only thinking, not sleeping. And, as usual, Batchelor wished to know what these thoughts were. This same curiosity had kept him loyal to Alva for twenty years – the thrilling anticipation of the next product to spring from that wonderful mind: for few were born and walked the earth who brought anything useful out of the flux of mental activity, and only a handful made the result beneficial to all.

Yet, it hurt him to see Alva like this, to think of the mysterious decline of the last three years, all the money ever earned thrown into a great hole in the ground. Stepping closer, Batch was even more disturbed to see that Alva's grimy duster was not in fact moving in the breeze, but had a life of its own: teeming with caterpillars that fell every few seconds from a cottonwood overhead.

Edison stirred and rose to his feet, the bugs cascading onto the floor, but without turning to look at Batch, he went into his cabin, shutting the door. A hermit – Edison had turned into a hermit.

Batchelor mounted the rickety steps and rapped on the door with his cane.

When it was opened, it was not Edison who stood there, but a stranger: a tall, gaunt, unshaven, bedraggled man, who tucked his shirt into his trousers as he spoke:

"Who iss it? Misster Edisson doessn't wish to be dissturbed" The absence of front teeth created this sibilance.

"Charles Batchelor to see Mr Edison. If you would be so kind."

"Charles Batchelor, is*s* it?" A catarrhal cough was muffled by his fist. "Thank you."

"Yes*s* *s*sir. I'll *s*see if he is available to *s*speak with you. But he does*s*n't usually want to be interrupted when he'*s*s working."

High etiquette for such a low house, thought Batch. This grotesque welcome, this decrepit butler: he tried to keep a straight face. "Is that so? Well, I am familiar with that kind of response, but if you'll tell him Charles Batchelor is here, I'd be surprised if he doesn't wish to see me."

Totally unconvinced, the man shut the door and left Batch to wait many more minutes than was polite or necessary.

The door opened again. "You can *s*see him," said the man, and behind him a familiar voice barked: "Stand aside, Frankie, for this is the great Charles Batchelor, paying me a house call. Go and put some water on. Quickly."

The man scurried away as Edison, with a smile, emerged from the darkness to embrace his old partner. They gripped each other at arm's length, each beholding a grandfather.

The Monastery was a shambles. Inside, papers and books lay strewn as after a tornado. A desk held a tower of unwashed plates. Amid the rubble, Batch spotted a half-finished letter, no doubt to Mina. Mouse droppings could be seen in the corners of the room. On a rumpled cot lay a fat, morose dog.

"A pet, Alva?"

"Why not. I rescued him, starving by a roadside. I've decided to spoil him. He's blind in one eye. I give him anything he wants. I really do love pets, you know." He scratched the dog affectionately between the ears, then sat and began to speak of the mill and the problems that had befallen it, all under the watchful glances of the new assistant, who had come back in the meantime with a fuming kettle. Batchelor had the impression that this servant's role fell between that of a guard, keeping the world and its demands away, and that of a nurse, attending to all of Edison's needs. Batchelor moved his chair so that his back would be turned to the assistant.

When the inventor noticed this, he ordered more coffee. "Frankie. Go find some."

What a relief when the two old friends were alone.

"Who is that extraordinary fellow?" asked Batchelor.

"Oh, he's all right. You don't remember him?"

"Should I?"

"Batch!" Edison laughed. "He's the lost man."

Batchelor inclined his head like a budgerigar. "The lost man?"

"The fella I sent off to South America to find a new fibre, remember, when I was crazy for a better lamp filament than your carbonized cardboard horseshoe."

"*That's* the man?" Batchelor had forgotten all about the mythical expedition. "I remember him as a young man. He must be at least – what, sixty?"

"Forty-five. Only forty-five. All my fault. He had some nasty experiences. All my fault. He was a schoolmaster, you know, before he came to me. I thought I'd killed him by sending him off on that wild-goose chase."

Edison bit off a plug of tobacco and offered Batchelor some. The guest turned it down.

"It all came out of my obsession to beat Westinghouse, y'see. So hell-bent on a superior lamp which could only run on direct current, remember? So when Frankie volunteered, I made him circumnavigate the globe for me. Ordered him to China, to Japan, India, Ceylon, Nepal – oh, God, to Bhutan, Burma, darn near everywhere – looking for exotic grasses that might serve as a filament. What was wrong with me, Batch? Had a period of inhumanity. The pilot light went out. Anyway, by telegram I even got him to cross the Andes into Peru, and to travel by donkey into Ecuador, then by riverboat to Colombia. He kept wiring back, saying he'd almost drowned in an Amazonian deluge or been attacked by mosquitoes the size of wasps. He begged for the money to come home, but I refused to send it to him, only tickets for somewhere new. I told him he had to find a fibre for me that wouldn't burn out, otherwise he couldn't come home. And after a year he even sent me a consignment of an elephantine grass, found only in the darkest reaches of the Colombian jungle, which grows to eighty feet. Incredible stuff. But utter waste of time as a filament. By then Frankie had come down with malaria. I didn't know how to reach him, so I forgot about him. Got lost in my own battle with Westinghouse. The whole chair business. That is, until I remembered of him soon after I came up here. I didn't do right by him, I kept thinking. So I sent people out to find him. Find if he was still alive, and make it up to him if he was. So I got a Pinkerton man, fella by the name of Billy Burns. For three months Burns couldn't find neither hide nor hair. That fella retraced Frankie's journey in reverse, starting in Colombia, but in the end that was where he found him. The tall grass had hidden Frankie pretty good. He was in a convent hospital with dysentery and pneumonia and half crazy. He wanted to be known as – guess who? – Billy Vanderbilt. Ha! When he was able to travel, I got him shipped back home, and ever since then I've looked after him because, as you can see, he's still not completely right these days. All my fault. Anyway, he's my new assistant, the new Charles Batchelor."

The real Batchelor had to smile. Insanity: was it now a prerequisite for employment with the new Edison?

It was time now to speak of his own mission: "So, Al, the reason I'm here. This is serious. How about coming back with me? Come with me, today."

"Today? Back?"

"This afternoon. There's another train at three. Give this up. Close this place down. There's no demand for ore of this grade, at any price – there never really was."

"It's closed down already. Can't you tell?"

"Then come back with me. Come back and straighten things out. I'll help you pack. Come on." Batch looked about him. "Shouldn't take us long."

Edison shook his head. "Not today."

"Why not? The ore mine is—"

Alva gave the same laugh Batchelor had first heard in the doorway of the American Telegraph Works in New York twenty years before. "Not today."

"Your family. They're waiting for you."

"You don't understand, Batch."

"Mina said—"

"All my fault there. I won't stand to see her miserable again."

"Isn't she miserable already? She wants you home."

"I won't turn her into another Mary. I'm dangerous, Batch. Lethal to be around."

"I talked to her. She wants you back."

His surprise increased. "You saw her?" His body straightened and, for a moment, he came back to life.

"Yes I did. And oh, before I forget, she has a message for you."

"A message? Really? What is it?"

"She wouldn't tell me. She wants to tell you herself. You have to go back and ask her yourself. This is what I was told to tell you."

A weary smile crossed Edison's face. "I see what she's playing at."

"I don't think she's playing any more, Al."

"No. Maybe not." Edison began to brood.

Batch was determined that the next words should be Alva's and he didn't stir, not even when Frankie brought back more coffee in two enamel mugs.

"Frankie," Edison said, "meet Charles Batchelor. My oldest friend and collaborator. Without him I couldn't have invented a darn thing. No phonograph. No light bulb. See, I never had any scientific training, no mathematics, no physics. And you really can't go very far without *them*."

The man nodded as he set down the mugs.

Batch was heartened. "I think that's almost the first time you've ever said something like that."

"Well, it's the living truth."

Blushing, Batch changed tack. So unaccustomed to praise was he, so deprived of renown, that he had lost the knack entirely for receiving compliments.

Edison sipped the bitter coffee, warmed his hands around the mug. "Ah, Batch... we did some things, didn't we? But y'know, one thing we never did was... well, we never managed to bring anyone back."

"Back?"

"From the dead."

Batchelor raised his eyebrows.

"Remember that dead mouse we thought we'd revived with 10,000 volts?"

Batch nodded. He remembered this, as he remembered everything.

"Well, Batch, I finally succeeded."

"*Succeeded?*"

"I brought Frankie here back from the dead – didn't I, Frankie?" Edison's smile brought a flicker of a response to the assistant's face.

"Good then," Batchelor said, seizing on this as his cue. "Then maybe you can pass the secret on to me, because the art of bringing

someone back from the dead just happens to be my current assign-
ment as well."

Edison roared. Even Frankie chuckled in his toothless, pathetic way,
before rising and leaving the room.

* * *

The train brought the two men slowly back to West Orange.

When they walked through the front door of *Glenmont*, Mina was
upstairs. Margarita Sanabria went white and flew up the stairs to
alert her mistress.

Edison remained in the hallway, waiting, like an uninvited guest in
a strange house, while Batch discreetly slipped into the living room.

To take off his dirty boots he sat on the low bench below the coat
rail. Under his children's coats, he tugged at the encrusted laces and
noted that Dot's pretty slippers were now the size of a young lady's,
while Dash's shoes were bigger than his own. The sight was a big
blow – and a new level of wretchedness came over him.

And then Mina appeared at the top of the stairs. He rose to his
feet. Her elegant dress suggested a certain readiness for his return.
They regarded each other across the expanse of the flight. "And who
do we have here?" she asked.

"Your husband, Ma'am. If you'll still have him."

She came down the stairs with a look of mature seriousness on her
face. "Will you stay for dinner at least?" Her tone was premeditated.
While he'd been gone, she had built a life for herself, built up a household, and had settled on a compromise which worked for her. Both
knew he had broken so many of the promises he had made during
their lakeside courtship that a new basis for a shared life had to be
found, and she wished to show him that she had found one.

"For dinner? Yes, I think I can stay that long."

"Then... I shall see you then." And with this she spun and passed into the dining room, where she began at once to instruct the cook on the precise order of the courses. The little he knew about women was that they were seldom so dismissive and cold unless they harboured emotions which were still not settled, which were still alive and might yet be stoked up. Through a crack in the door he watched her point at the candelabra, gesture for the flowers to be moved. She was telling him that their life together would now be on her terms. That was the message she had for him after his long absence. And it did not require words.

THOMAS

Life was surely leaking out of the inventor. Alone on the platform, he felt the dead close by. And yet, with reserves still to call on, his memory refused to burn out.

In drifting, soaring states he saw new evidence that the memory survives the body. Undimmed even now were these indestructible thought pictures, his old recordings, as vivid as ever, maybe even more so as the body failed: after all, what is an old man but a memory machine?

Alive then, *in vacuo*, these life records, long-chambered, seemed to be awaiting the moment when the vacuum would fail, to take flight and swarm free over land and sea, to circumnavigate the cosmos until, one day, they would settle again – rationality demands it – on some random thing, perhaps a child, some innocent somewhere who has a higher thought, one far beyond his or her own experience, and wonders where on earth it came from.

> *Scattered like dust and leaves, when the mighty blasts of October*
> *Seize them, and whirl them aloft, and sprinkle them far o'er the ocean.*

And now, with his eyes shut, better to concentrate on the life that was left to him, he dispatched a late thought to Nikola Tesla. *Tesla, what of you now? Living it up at the Waldorf Astoria for so many years on Morgan's money – money you used to build a ludicrous tower with which to turn the earth into a vast dynamo by transmitting high-frequency electricity all round the globe, free and available to all. When Morgan finally understood that your electricity would be free, he withdrew his money. Tesla, the world, it does not know what to do with genius, but we should not have been enemies.*

And Morgan. *What of you? Where, old goat, did we leave the world after all? Was the honour and trust we borrowed from the public repaid?*

"Morgan Dead," the headlines had announced in 1913. The cause? A *combination*: this time of strokes and a nervous breakdown. He had died angry, depressed, delusional. For a while there, twenty years after the Eighties, Morgan's star rose and rose. But in the end the world smelt a rat. Something had to be done about a system which managed the masses so callously. The antitrust movement sprang up after 1910 to smash his combines, but he had built them too well. His corporations would continue to govern most of the globe. His was a story of success. Still, the mere suggestion that he had done wrong took its toll on him. Edison recalled the widely reported 1912 congressional hearings into the monopoly practices of various bankers and banks, which had treated Morgan, finally, like a villain.

COUNSEL: State your name.
MORGAN: John Pierpont Morgan.
COUNSEL: Sir, you have been called the "Boss of the United States".
MORGAN: I've been called many things.

How imposing Morgan had looked in those last twelve months of his life – and never more so than on that morning as he had steered himself through the streets of Washington DC, dressed all in black (to the end a dazzling fast walker, the cane in swift use), overcoat buttoned only at the top, its tails flaring like a cape, flanked by his daughter and son, scattering pigeons and onlookers who had come to catch a glimpse of this man reported to head an empire comprising 341 directorships which controlled some $22 billion in resources and capitalization. How seldom could he be seen at large – having long adopted the most seclusive ways. But here he was, his nose ghastly, his forehead knotted in a scowl, his face taut and strained.

COUNSEL: Will you admit, sir, that you preside over a banking system that has seen this country exposed to two decades of brutal mergers and a carnival atmosphere on Wall Street which has triggered booms and busts in insane succession?

MORGAN (*over jeers from the gallery*): No! This is false. Character. (*Thumps his cane on the ground loudly*) Before money, before everything else, there is character. The first thing is character!

(*Counsel unveils a blackboard on which a diagram is pinned, illustrating Mr Morgan's interconnected concerns: a complex map of great and small companies all orbiting, planet-like, J.P. Morgan & Co.*)

COUNSEL: I ask you again, sir. Will you admit that you and the six major banking houses under your influence essentially control, unchecked and without supervision, the flow of credit in this country?

MORGAN (*over applause*): It may be true that at present we have a small number of very powerful banking houses in this land, but… they are likely to be far less potent as the years go on.

(*Hoots from the crowd*)

COUNSEL: Does Wall Street speculation, Mr Morgan, draw a great deal of money from the country?

MORGAN: I think so. Yes.

COUNSEL: Would you favour any legislation that would reduce the volume of speculation?

MORGAN: No.

COUNSEL: You would let speculation run riot?

(*Morgan pauses, but only briefly*)

MORGAN: Yes.

(*Crowd, an uncontrolled outburst over the following*)

MORGAN: You want… you want a human sacrifice here! A Martyr. You have chosen me, and turned on me like dogs. But I am not your enemy. I'm not your enemy!

Even in the dock, with the evidence before him, he could not see why the public was so angry at him. He saw himself only as a saviour, at the very least honourable, and the cartoons that appeared around the world of him with a devil's tail dealt him a vicious blow.

In Washington, the congressional committee pronounced him guilty of a kind of treason: J.P. Morgan and five other houses were found to be running the US economy for their own benefit, crushing anything "that threatened their relentless growth". The shock of this censure killed him. Within a year he was dead. The obituaries contained pictures of the $500 suite in Rome where he had met his end, the lobby teeming with art dealers trying to offload a last painting, statue or manuscript. The Romans loved him for his spending. The Pope wrote a eulogy. Ships at sea flew ensigns at half-mast when word came. Stock exchanges closed. He was mourned like an Emperor. Greed, it seemed, could be honoured too. In his time he had donated widely, and these investments paid late dividends. It turned out that the public, consumers after all, had consumed J.P. Morgan's faults as well.

On the dilapidated platform the inventor remembered only too well that he had also benefited from the public's appetite for the faults of fabulous men and women. A week after the Kemmler affair, his own role in it had largely been forgotten. But he was tougher on himself than that, and he still wondered if the part he had played had been evil. If the evil person is one who can only be happy when making

other people unhappy, then he had never fallen *that* low. But still…
As the years passed, the Kemmler incident had not dimmed for him,
but rather had become linked in his mind with the invention of the
incandescent lamp – twin memories: one negative, the other positive, forming a closed circuit through which the currents of the past
flowed without end.

He opened his eyes on the platform. Was he alive? Yes, he was still
functioning. The heart still beating, the mind sending out its mad
signals. With a handkerchief he mopped his brow and sensed again, as
he had his entire life, the unborn ideas still inside him, ideas superior
to anything he'd ever grasped. What might he have achieved had he
been a more sensitive receptor for divine secrets? At the same time,
he recognized that he would never now take hold of these tantalizing
works, for ever just beyond his reach. He sighed at the realization
that we finally produce only a fraction of what we are capable of,
and will be remembered at best for our brightest failures.

Still, this was perhaps the common fate, and with no time left for
his soul to find a better conductor than the brain he'd been given,
he had no choice but to stand by his trifles, to accept with dignity
the public salutes and, for the sake of his name, pretend to the end
to have been one of the chosen, one of the few to have ever spied
through a crack in the eternal door and glanced for a moment the
mysteries of the sacred illumination.

He felt a vibration in the broad pine planks of the platform floor.
Lowering his head, he clamped his teeth on the stock of his cane. Yes,
a train. Definitely a train. Coming back for him. His time was up.

* * *

Mina was the first to appear through the train's steam – the first, as
usual, to find him. She approached with a smile. "Deary, we lost you."

Yes, the perfect phrase. For so long he had been lost to himself. But if she was angry, she hid it well. A certain delinquency was expected of the aged, and even if everyone guessed he'd done his best to sabotage his own jubilee, to the extent of inconveniencing a president, it was unlikely to be mentioned. To do so would only further mar the day. "ARE YOU ALL RIGHT?"

"One hundred decibels, no more."

"So this is how you gave us the slip! Stepping off your own ceremonial train! Keep the President of the United States and half of Wall Street waiting!"

"A day to remember." He looked into the face that always turned him back to the human race. "I... had to... catch my breath."

She leant closer. "We were almost about to pull up in Dearborn when we discovered you weren't on the train. Do you have any idea how hard it was to reverse a train all this way? Henry Ford is very annoyed. You've ruined his choreography."

"Rats."

"We were worried. When we found your private car empty, Marie Curie said you'd ascended to heaven in bodily form."

"I can't face them, Mina."

"Who? Hoover? J.P. Morgan?" When Edison glanced swiftly at her she corrected herself. "The son." And seeing his confusion continue even then, "J.P. Morgan Junior, deary. Oh, you should see them. Bands, music, oh Tom! Fifty years since the electric lamp was born – you can't disappoint them. Come on, let's get back on the train, please."

Edison looked away: the memory machine was turning once more. "Where did we leave it, Pierpont? The world?"

"Don't waste your energies, Tom."

But he had a need now to tell her what had been on his mind. Pointing to Dearborn with his stick, and with anger surfacing: "He got his way, though. Got his marriage majestical. And today's the wedding anniversary. Well, I wanna divorce. Send the bankers home."

"Shh. Shhh now. Calm down. Stop this. We are all going to Dearborn together."

"You go on, go to Dearborn. Pick me up here on the way back. Say I fell ill. Sick in the head."

"Tom! Don't be foolish. Just be calm."

"I fell short, Mina. A long way short. I prided myself on my *virtue*. But the pilot light went out. See, they don't tell ya – nobody tells ya – that when you do a wrong, that nothing, nothing on this earth burns so bright and attractive as the next wrong just waiting to be done."

"Shh now. It's lovely up ahead. Wait and see."

But he wasn't done yet. His heart still ached with anger, and Edison was again pierced with the pain brought on by his memories. He roared: "You know what I'm talking about!"

And just as fiercely, for she knew now how to match him, and sometimes even to exceed him in passion: "But we don't have to discuss it! Remember? We don't talk about it!"

"But I have to talk about it! I have to talk about it! I did things, Mina – I set – set things in motion there's no stopping now! Three million years to make a steam engine, just fifty more to electrify a city, and now, every week some revolution. Oh, humanity's all fired up now, spitting out smoke and sparks – and there I was, feeding the furnaces, throwing the switches..." He caught his breath. Was it his heart? She stepped closer, ready to support him if he fell. "What year?" he asked, his energies spent. "What year is this?"

"1929. It's 1929, Deary." Louder: "August 1929."

"Terrible times."

"Terrible? They're boom times."

"Who knows what's up ahead. What's coming. Undo the experiments, that's what I say. Shatter the inventions. Give us back the dark."

This was too much for Mina. She took his arm tightly. "Thomas! You can't meet everybody like this. DO YOU HEAR ME?" With a handkerchief she wiped his shining brow. And finally his rage gave way. A heavy defeated sigh came from his chest. "What's come over you?" she asked. "All right, take a moment, Deary. Shhh now. Sit." Steering him to the bench, they sat side by side. "There. There now. Come on." This man, her husband, was dying before her eyes, but she had to remain strong. She looked about her for the first time. A red sky was coming up beyond the spare austere plains. "It's beautiful here."

And at this point another woman appeared on the platform. Young. Wearing the fashion of the previous century. Carrying no luggage. Edison knew at once where he'd seen her before. How familiar she was! "You're angry at me," he said, as the new woman crossed slowly towards him without a word to sit on the opposite side of him from Mina. "I did a great wrong. Wasn't listening hard enough, was I?…"

Mina put her hand on his, which held the cane. "Tom?"

"No," he added.

"Thomas? Listen to me now. Are you listening? Listen" – at which she lifted his hand and began to tap with his cane on the boards.

His eyes widened.

When she had finished tapping she asked, "Did it make sense?"

Visibly moved, he nodded. "And do you? Do you forgive me?"

She leant close to his ear, so he couldn't fail to hear: "I do" and then, "We *all* do".

He took in these words, took them in deeply. "I waited a long time. To be wired those three words."

"A long time? But we were only gone ten minutes."

Mina rose on his right side, and as she did so Edison saw that the silent young woman on his left rose as well.

"Come now," Mina said. "Everyone's waiting for you. When we stopped to come back for you we could hear them chanting."

"What? What were they chanting? The people. The public. Are they mocking me?"

She helped him to his feet. "No. They're saying... 'Let there be light. Let there be light.' Can you hear them? Listen. That's what they're saying. 'Let there be light.'"

She led him towards the train.

"You're sure?" he asked. "Sure that's what they're chanting? Make sure."

"They want to thank you, Tom. For the boom. Their wealth. Their good fortune. Now come."

As they came close to the ceremonial train, a puff of steam briefly filled the platform and closed in all around them. They stopped and waited for a moment, and when the steam dissipated the old man could no longer see the other woman.

"Let there be light?" he finally said, on the move once more, as he had always, always been on the move. "Yes. That's fine. Let there be light."

"Oh, Tom – isn't it wonderful?"

AUTHOR'S NOTE

Although this story is drawn from the available facts, it hasn't been my intention to provide a new biographical record of the life of T.A.E. My approach is as rigorous – no more, no less – than an old person's reconstruction of their own past, a work of memory, prone to amplifications, editorializing and compression. I take as justification for this approach Edison's own restructuring of his own life story. As one of his biographers, Robert Conot, notes: "His memory was almost dateless." As ever, the writer of a fiction based on fact relies on the discerning reader to weigh the two commodities.

I'm indebted to the Edison Papers Project at Rutgers University and to the Pierpont Morgan Library, as well as biographers and historians, notably Neil Baldwin, Craig Brandon, Ron Chernow, Robert Conot, Paul Israel, Matthew Josephson, T.H. Metzger and Jean Strouse. Compared to their scholarly labours I did no more than swirl a teacup and watch a story suggest itself in the leaves.

Lastly, I dedicate this book to my editor, and friend, Alessandro Gallenzi.

– Anthony McCarten